Leslie Cope Cornford

Captain Jacobus

Leslie Cope Cornford

Captain Jacobus

ISBN/EAN: 9783337075767

Printed in Europe, USA, Canada, Australia, Japan

Cover: Foto ©Andreas Hilbeck / pixelio.de

More available books at **www.hansebooks.com**

CAPTAIN JACOBUS

BY

L. COPE CORNFORD

NEW YORK

STONE & KIMBALL

M DCCC XCVI

Contents

Contents

Captain Jacobus

—◆—

I

THE RIVALS

ONE March morning, in the year of our
Lord 1655, I mounted my horse at the
door of Langford Manor, and, filled with the
blithest anticipations, set forth to Salisbury City.
Such an occasion befalls a man but once in his
life, and it behooves him to make the most of it.
The weather was bright and sunny, with a merry
breeze that shook down the yellow catkins upon
man and beast as we passed : the countryside
appeared to laugh and sing ; and when I entered
the venerable city, it greeted me with a sparkling aspect whereto my eyes seemed newly
opened.

Leaving my horse at the sign of the Sun over
against the Conduit, in the High Street, I took

my way towards the Market Place, where, just beyond the Poultry Cross, stands the house of Mr. Richard Phelps, at that time Mayor of Salisbury. As luck would have it, I had scarce gone twenty paces from the inn before I saw John Manning advancing down the street. Now of all persons in the world I disliked Mr. Manning the worst : and I think he hated me ; but this morning (for the first time) I felt I could perfectly afford to be civil. For hitherto John Manning had always the upper hand of me in a manner of quiet domineering highly irksome to a generous nature. Our respective fathers, serving under the headlong leadership of Sir Harry Bard, were slain on Alresford field while I was still undergoing education at New College, Oxford. But young Manning, who was five years my senior, had fought side by side with his father, and had been wounded in the left arm and shoulder, — a misfortune of which he was most inordinately vain. Moreover, he was a very proper man, with a silver tongue and a pretty trick of using it ; while I, although greater of body, was a shy and plain youth, with no such mighty talent for conversation. Time and again, when I have been sitting

8

happily with Barbara, he has entered upon us and put me to the blush with his courtly performances, till I was fain to quit the room in the blackest of tempers.

As he came cocking down the pavement I perceived that Mr. Manning was dressed as if for a festival, in silver-laced silken coat, quilted breeches slashed with crimson, and silken stockings of the same color: he wore a silver-hilted walking-sword, and the black love-lock disposed upon his shoulder was tied with a knot of silver-pointed crimson ribbon.

"Well met, Anthony," cried Manning, stopping and holding out his hand. "You shall be the first to wish me joy this fine morning."

His greeting took me very much aback, for it was precisely the manner of address I had prepared in my own mind for Manning. Then it occurred to me that his attentions to Mistress Barbara Phelps had, after all, expressed no more than friendship; and I shook his proffered hand till the bones cracked, and my gallant had much ado to preserve an unmoved countenance.

"With all my heart," I said. "And who is the so fortunate lady?"

Manning smiled pleasantly. "I may not tell you her name," he replied. "For to say truth, I have won but the father's consent to my courtship. But I do not despair of the maiden's."

"Why here is a singular coincidence," I cried. "Give me your good wishes in turn, Manning, for I have the maiden's consent, and I am hoping for the father's."

Manning's face darkened suddenly. "Indeed!" said he. "And who is the so fortunate lady?"

His manner surprised me, and awoke a suspicion.

"Well, the affair is private, at present," I returned. "Nevertheless, I should think you might give a reasonable near guess."

"I profess myself at a loss," replied Manning, coldly.

"Why, then I will leave you to think over it at leisure. Give you good-den, Mr. Manning," and I made as if to go.

But Manning planted himself squarely across my path.

"And where are you going in such a mighty hurry, Mr. Anthony Langford?"

"What is that to you?" I retorted, losing patience, and attempting to push past him. "Out o' my way!"

Manning caught me by the arm. "It is this to me," he said, "that there is just one house in this city which I warn you not to visit, or you and I will fall out. Do not feign to misunderstand me, Anthony."

"I shall visit where I please," I said, wrenching my arm free. "What nonsense is this? Stand back, or I draw on you!"

I laid my hand on the hilt of my rapier, but Manning seized my wrist. The touch was as a match to powder, and I caught him a buffet on the point of the chin with my left hand. I heard his teeth click together like the snapping of a trap, and he loosed his hold and staggered backwards. I drew sword and stood on guard, expecting of course that Manning would attack me then and there. But seeing the people beginning to throng from all sides, my adversary thought better of it, and putting a laced kerchief to his mouth, he came up to me and slipped his arm through mine, as if we had been merely jesting.

"Put up your blade," he said in a low voice. "Do you want to get us both in jail, you madman?"

I had nothing to do but to comply, and we began to walk forward. The crowd followed us a little distance, but seeing there was no more sport to be had, presently dwindled away and left us to march arm-in-arm across the market-place.

"You forget yourself strangely at times, Mr. Langford," remarked Manning. "But be assured that I shall not forget you. And since you will not take advice, I am going to do myself the honor of accompanying you upon your visit."

"With all my heart," I returned. "And I beg you to remark that, for my part, I make no stipulation. It doth not appear to me a dignified proceeding."

Manning replied nothing, and we arrived in silence at the door of old Richard Phelps's tall, gabled mansion, with the squares of white plaster between the black cross-timbering and projecting diamond-paned windows. Before Manning could speak I had told the house-wench who ushered us into the long, low room on the first floor, to inform Mr. Phelps that Mr. Anthony Langford requested the honor of a few minutes' talk with him. A wood-fire crackled upon the hearth, for the weather was chilly ; and Manning and I stood stiffly side by side with our backs to the high mantelpiece. We were careful that our respective shoulders should not touch, by the fraction of an inch : had they done so, neither would have budged a hair's-breadth, and contention might have ensued. So we stood as rigid as a pair of statues until the door opened and Mr. Phelps entered the room. The Mayor was a broad-shouldered, ruddy, bald old gentleman, with twinkling blue eyes and a gray beard.

"Why, Anthony, my boy, how do you do ? What, back so soon, John ! Oons, what hast done to thy mouth, man ? Thou canst never go a-wooing in that guise. Or perhaps Barbara will help to make it well again, hey ?" and the old man winked genially at me.

I was resolved to take the lead in this three-cornered interview if I could, and before Manning could open his damaged lips I began.

"Mr. Phelps, I have come upon a personal affair of some delicacy, which I should have preferred to discuss with you in private. But as Mr. Manning has thought fit, for reasons of his own, to force himself upon my company, I can very well say what I have to say before him. I am come, sir, to request your permission to pay my addresses to your daughter, Mistress Barbara,'' I concluded, with hot cheeks, and lips that had suddenly become parched.

"I have had the honor to inform Mr. Langford of what passed between us this morning," Manning put in.

The Mayor comprehended us both in a glance that seemed to betoken some amusement.

"And so then you fell to fisticuffs, like a pair of school-boys? I am ashamed of you, gentlemen," said he; and Manning flushed darkly. "I will deal plainly with you," he went on. "One at a time is but fair play, Anthony. Had you got up a little more betimes, you would have had the start: now Manning has the advantage. I will have no brawling in my house, and since you cannot agree, you must wait till John has thrown his main. If he fails in his suit, why, you may come to me again. I will favor neither of you

by so much as a word. 'T is for Barbara to
choose : she shall do as she likes ; and so long as
she is happy, you will find her father pleased,"
concluded this exemplary parent.

This was what I desired, and a great weight
lifted from my mind at his words ; for I had
been sore afraid that Mr. Phelps was set upon
Manning for a son-in-law. Nevertheless, I did
not see why Barbara should be cumbered with
Manning's odious courtesies for an indefinite
period.

"Nothing can be fairer, and whatever befall, I am much beholden to your kindness," I
said. "But how long must I wait my turn,
sir ?"

"Nay, that you must ask John Manning,"
said the old man.

"Mr. Manning's manner of conversation
does not gratify me," I replied. "I had rather
ask Mistress Barbara. Your daughter has been
acquainted with both Mr. Manning and myself
from childhood, and if she hath taken a fancy
to either, doubtless her mind is settled."

Manning must have known himself defeated,
but he played a last card.

"Perhaps Mr. Langford has his own reasons for such a supposition," he struck in, and despite all I could do, I felt myself flush.

Old Phelps looked sharply at me, and his face grew stern.

"What have you to say to that, Anthony?" he asked.

"It is true," said I, "and a breach of proper etiquette, I own. But it only occurred last night. I am instant to repair it, you see, sir."

"You did very wrong, sir," returned the outraged father, angrily. "Here is a pretty state of affairs. It would serve you right were I to forbid you the house."

"I demand it," cried Manning. "Your pledge to me admits of no other course, Mr. Phelps."

"Does it not?" said the old gentleman, who was perhaps glad to find another outlet for his anger. "But I am not accustomed to take orders, John Manning, and I think differently. Come, we will settle this matter off-hand!" and opening the door he shouted, "Barbara!"

Manning, seeing what was to follow, went as white as a clout, and catching up his hat, strode towards the open door.

"I fear I shall spoil your little plot, but I have no fancy to be made a show of," said he. "I have fallen into a strange mistake, it seems; but 't is not too late to amend it. Give your good-den, Mr. Mayor," and before the astonished old man could answer, my rival was gone.

He must have passed Barbara on the stairs, for she entered almost immediately. My betrothed dwelt ever in my thoughts: and when we were absent from each other, I would please myself by picturing in my mind her look when we should meet again; and still, when it came to pass, her beauty struck me always newly, in a kind of revelation. So it was upon her entrance that morning, with her shining hair and blue eyes, apparelled in something checkered and dainty of the same color.

"Prithee, father, what's the matter?" asked Barbara.

"Matter!" said Mr. Phelps. "Why, the matter is, that, whereas this morning you had a couple of sweethearts, now you have only the one. Will he content ye, my dear?"

"We can but try, at all events," said Barbara.

It was late that night before I found myself riding homeward under the stars. My way lay across the old bridge that spans the river Avon, where a little islet, upon which is built a chapel, stems the mid-stream. The roadway of the bridge passes underneath groined arches which carry the chapel floor: on either side a stairway rises to an open balcony, which, running right round the building, and fenced by a stone balustrading of foliated open-work, gives access to the interior. The moonlight glittered upon the swirling flood below, and sparkled here and there, amid the elaborate confusion of flying buttresses and pinnacles, upon the tall windows of the chapel.

Riding at a footpace across the bridge, I had come within a bow's shot of the archway, when a horseman leaped from the black shadow and came charging towards me. I had scarce time to note the glint of steel in his right hand ere he was upon me. Hardly knowing what I did, I slipped from my saddle to avoid his onset. The rider swerved, but I dodged and ran for the chapel, as man and horse collided with my own steed. I heard a mighty clatter of hoofs upon the stones behind me, and my horse galloped past just as I reached the archway. The moment's delay saved me. A dismounted man has little chance against a horseman, and I took no shame to myself for running away.

I sprang up the winding steps, and had reached the balcony, when I heard the echoing clang of hoofs. Peering over the coping, I perceived the road on the further side of the chapel to be empty ; my pursuer had therefore dismounted, and was probably at that very moment ascending one or other of the two staircases, pistol in hand. I had not seen his face, for it was masked with a black vizard and muffled, but I could think of no one who bore me such a deadly grudge as this appeared to indicate, save Manning. He should find me ready for him this bout, at any rate. I drew my sword (a long Italian rapier), and, taking off my horseman's cloak, wrapped it twice round my left arm, grasping the collar in my hand, allowing a yard or so of the skirt to hang loose. Going to the top of the steps, I listened intently.

There was no sound save the stamping of the impatient horse below and the jingling of his bit, so that Manning must have chosen to escalade the fortress by the opposite stairs.

I reflected, with some emotion, that my enemy doubtless had pistols, whilst I had none. Nevertheless, I had no intention of being stalked like a beast, and treading noiselessly to the angle buttress, laid my cheek to the stone, and stole a glance round the corner. Sure enough, there was Manning, with a naked rapier in one hand and a long pistol in the other, advancing with the most excessive caution. The moon shone full upon his upturned face, so that I could see the whites of his eyes behind the black mask, and the lips beneath the bristling mustachio curling from the clenched teeth like the snarl of a dog, as he lifted and noiselessly put down first one foot and then the other.

It was my turn to charge this time, and I dashed out upon him. The suddenness of my onset caused him to shoot wide with his maimed arm, as I had hoped and prayed, and I heard the bullet sing past my head. Manning thereupon thrust at me swiftly, but with an old trick of the fencing-school I entangled his blade in my heavy cloak, and catching the hilt with my left hand, tore it from his grasp, at the same time lunging forward till my right foot was behind my adversary's back. He was thus at my mercy; but I had never killed a man at that time, and my blood turned from the deed. I have never ceased to regret my surrender to that womanish impulse. As it was, I girt him round the lower ribs, and began to squeeze the breath out of him. Manning sobbed and struggled and swore, but his arms were pinioned, and I was the stronger man. So soon as he was quiet I let him drop, and he lay gasping. Then I picked up his sword and snapped it across my knee: his pistols I stuck in my belt, and stood a paternoster-while to fetch my breath.

"Look you, John Manning," I said presently. "We will call quits, and no squares broke. But I have just one word to say. Mark me, if ever I meet you within sight of Salisbury Cathedral spire again, may I be judged by the Four Evangelists, but I will fight you. You had best be packing before daylight, for I am about pretty betimes. I wish you joy, John Manning."

Captain Jacobus

With that I left him, and started to walk to Langford Manor : but I had not gone far before I came upon my horse, cropping the hedge ; and mounting, I rode home, and so to bed, to dream of Barbara.

II

CAPTAIN JACOBUS

NEXT day, and for several days afterwards, I rose very betimes to transact the affairs of my estate with my steward, then rode away hotfoot to Salisbury, to the house of Mayor Phelps. Looking back upon that brief period of felicity, I see a rich procession of sunny hours, musical with the falling chimes of the towering Cathedral, during which we found such happiness that I sometimes felt afraid. I could not think that I had earned such fortune, and I doubted whether God would allow it ; and, indeed, after-events put some color on this reasoning.

My betrothed was an only child : her father, old Richard Phelps, was a master cutler, and (so it was said) had amassed a pretty fortune in his business. How much it was I did not know, and took no pains to discover ; but when we came to discuss marriage settlements, the old man told me he would dower his daughter with three thousand pounds. My own estate of Langford Manor, although much impaired and impoverished during the Civil Wars, was yet sufficient ; and there seemed no reason why we should not marry out of hand. But Barbara, it appeared, had a great equipment of garments to buy or to make ; and although I could never apprehend the force of the argument, some delay appeared inevitable. At length, however, the wedding was settled for the 18th of April, and, like a schoolboy, I put up a calendar over my bed's head, and scored out a date every morning. And in my voyages to and fro I rode very circumspectly, in case some accident should befall me.

There was scarce a month to run before the day appointed, when destiny fulfilled my fearful expectations at a blow. Riding homeward in the moonlight across country, as I topped the bare down that shelters Langford village I was aware of a horseman galloping along the ridge towards me. Remembering Mr. Manning's former exploit, I drew rein, and, putting myself in a posture of defence, awaited the rider, who thereupon slackened speed, so that I had time to observe him as he drew near. But the stranger was a smaller man than Manning, bestriding a huge roan horse, and carrying an arquebus slung across his shoulders, besides pistols in his holsters, and a French riding-sword.

"I have the honor to address Mr. Anthony Langford, of Langford Manor, I believe?" said he, reining up and removing his black montero-cap, with a very courtly gesture.

"At your service, sir," I replied, saluting him in turn. The stranger had a quick military manner of utterance, and before the words were out of my mouth he continued earnestly: —

"Then will you do me the favor, Mr. Langford, to ride with me a little way? I have somewhat to say to you. Oh, yes," he added, as I hesitated, "y'are perfectly right: I am a highwayman, 't is true; but I am not here to rob you, nevertheless. Why, you and I have met before, sir. Have you forgotten Captain Jacobus?"

I had not; and now I knew why I remembered mistily the square, strong face, with its

great jaw and long nose hooking over the curling mustachio. For one night, before my
mother died, she and I were driving homewards in our great family coach over the downs.
I was barely in my teens, but I could fence a
bit, and shoot at a mark; and sitting by my
mother, with my arm round her waist as the
huge vehicle swung and jolted over the ruts,
and my little sword between my knees, I felt
myself a match for a whole band of robbers.
But I must have forgotten my wardship and
fallen on sleep, for I awoke with a start, as the
coach stopped suddenly, to see the dark figure
of a horseman abreast of the window. My
mother bade me sit still; and the highwayman
swung himself from his horse and leaned over
the sill.

"Madam," he began, but got no further,
for my mother cried out in astonishment.

"Sir Clipseby Carew!" she exclaimed.

"No, not now," he returned. "Captain
Jacobus, Alicia, at your service."

They conversed together for a while in the
French tongue, a language of which I had but
small understanding; then the Captain kissed

my mother's hand, and rode away into the night. When I asked my mother who was the strange man, she told me how Sir Clipseby Carew was an old friend of hers ; and how the Parliament-men had robbed him of his estates, obliging him to change his name and to take to the road for a living, like many another Cavalier at that unhappy time. The incident engraved itself upon my boyish imagination, so that for a long time the Captain used often to ride through the mazes of my dreams ; and ever since, rumors of his exploits had reached my ears from time to time, and kept the remembrance green. Recalling all this, I was glad enough to put up my pistol, and turning my horse's head, to jog along beside Captain Jacobus.

"Why, now I remember, and I am glad indeed to renew my acquaintance with Sir Clipseby Carew," I said.

"'T is long since I heard the title," he returned, twisting his mustache. "But other days are coming, we 'll hope. Will you join us, Mr. Langford, to help regain the King his own ?"

"Well, I am a King's man, sure enough," I

answered. "But the fact is, Captain, I am going to be married. I do not want to meddle in broils and insurrections."

"You do not?" returned the Captain. "Why, then, what else have you been doing of late, Mr. Langford?"

"Unless a-preparing for wedlock be an offence against the Protector, I do not know," I said in surprise.

"You have no hand in the plot, then?"

"On the rood, no! What plot?"

"Then why are Crook's dragoons billeted in Langford Manor House?" asked the Captain. "And why are patrols posted along the Salisbury Road to lag you by the heels?"

"What!" I cried, reining up. I knew Captain Crook very well by repute for a zealous servant of Ironside's, who patrolled a district of the West Country with a troop of horse.

"Don't stop, man. We can talk as we're going. Well, I thought you knew naught of it, and that was the reason I stopped you. Your estates are confiscate, young man, and you yourself outlawed, as like as not. I don't know why, but there it is, you see."

Captain Jacobus

The blow had fallen, then. I thought of Barbara, and our towering hopes toppled into the dust. Then I felt the Captain's hand on my shoulder for a moment, and his rough exhortation rang in my ears.

"Bear up! What, man! worse has happened to better men. We'll be upsides with the bloody regicides before all's done. Come! take the road with me, and 'list yourself into Sir John Penruddock's volunteers; we want men of your inches. This is no time for marrying. Wait until the King is cocking it at Whitehall, and then you can marry as much as you please."

"I must go to Salisbury first," I cried.

"Do you desire your sweetheart to behold her lover's head aloft on Chapel Bridge, a-sundrying on a pike-end?" inquired the Captain, grimly. "But you may send her a letter by a messenger of mine to-night," he added.

"But what have I done? Why should I, as peaceable a citizen as God ever made, be suddenly clapped up for a traitor?"

"How should I know?" replied the Captain. "The point is, I take it, that so it is, most unmistakably. Hast quarrelled with any one who hath the ear of Cromwell, or that bloody spider Secretary Thurloe, by any chance ?"

"I have quarrelled with no man, excepting Mr. John Manning, and he is a Royalist and a Catholic."

"Ah!" said Captain Jacobus; "and how was that ?"

Whereupon I related the story of our difference, without of course mentioning the lady's name.

"And you have not fallen across him since ?" inquired Jacobus, when I had finished.

"No."

"Well, Mr. Langford, if you get a man stark mad with jealousy under your hand, and then you let him go free (and why you did so passeth my poor imagination), you must not be astonished at disaster. That is all there is to be said. And now to the business in hand, — which is the only thing that can help you, or any of us, in this distraught realm."

There seemed nothing for it but to follow the Captain's leading ; and with a heart as heavy as lead I resigned myself to fate. As we trotted steadily forward, Captain Jacobus told me the main outlines of the conspiracy against the Lord Protector then kindling throughout the North and West, in which the tried Cavalier at my side was a principal agent.

The Earl of Rochester, it appeared, was then in London, living very private, awaiting intelligence from Sir Marmaduke Darcy, who was gathering forces in the North, and from Sir John Penruddock and Sir Joseph Wagstaff, who were the West Country leaders. Captain Jacobus had appointed to meet the two latter gentlemen that night, in order to receive their instructions, which he was straightway to carry to Rochester, who was in communication with the King. All things, in our part of the country, were prepared for an immediate rising. It only remained to fix the date, which must be done by the King, who was at that moment lying secretly upon the Flemish coast, ready to cross should occasion so require.

"That is the complexion of affairs," concluded the Captain. "Now will you join us, Mr. Langford, for good or evil fortune? And I warn you, I that have seen the beginning and sad end of more than one such hopeful enterprise, 'tis but the spin of a coin betwixt defeat and victory.''

The first shock of my dire misfortune was passing, and I began to feel mighty angry, and a very fervent rebel.

" Well, I am art and part with you ! " I cried, and we shook hands as we rode.

So there was I, upon the eve of marriage and the leisurely, pastoral life of a country gentleman, pitchforked into I knew not what hugger-mugger of civil broils, setting my life and Barbara's happiness upon the hazard of a cast. Well, it had to be, and I must make the best of it. But I resolved that I would cut Mr. Manning's throat the next time fortune brought us to meet.

By this time, after fetching a compass, we had arrived at Wilton, an ancient hamlet about five miles west of Salisbury, where, at the sign of the Orle of Martlets (the cognizance of the Earls of Pembroke), Captain Jacobus had appointed to meet Sir John Penruddock and the gentlemen associated with him. We found the company assembled together in an upper room of the inn, the most of whom were smoking long pipes, with glasses of liquor in front of them upon the shining oaken table. Captain Jacobus introduced me to Colonel Sir John Penruddock, a tall, dark, grave gentleman, with something of a visionary look about him; and to Major-General Sir Joseph Wagstaff, a red, round, turkey-cock of a man. They bade us be seated and filled our glasses.

I remarked then, for the first time, what I often had occasion to note afterwards, how the Captain, in some unobtrusive and undefinable way, assumed precedence in whatsoever company he found himself, even among men who had the habit of command. I have since put it down to his magnificent self-confidence, a quality which sets the seal, in the world's eye, upon the charter of man's worth.

" Well, Sir John," began Captain Jacobus, briskly, " what tidings for his Lordship ? "

" Tell the Earl of Rochester that we in Wiltshire can put a troop of two hundred horse into the field at a day's notice, and the Hampshire people as many. We are only waiting for my Lord to appoint the day and the place."

" Why, very well," returned the Captain. " I will ride to-night."

A short conversation ensued, in which it was

arranged, amongst other matters, that I should ride with the Captain ; whereat, in my consuming zeal for action, I was well content.

"No stopping of coaches full of fine ladies this journey, Captain!" said Sir Joseph Wagstaff, with a chuckle. He was sitting at ease, with his buff coat flung open and his fine lawn shirt ruffling out like plumage. "I am sorry for you, my excellent friend, but the King's interests before all!"

"Is the King not interested in ladies, then, my Joseph?" inquired the Captain.

Sir Joseph was gathering his forces for a reply when Sir John Penruddock, rising, interrupted him.

"Gentlemen," cried the Colonel, "fill your glasses. A toast before we part. Gentlemen — the King! God bless him, and may he speedily enjoy his own again!"

I have drunk the King's health many a time since then, — even at his Majesty's own table, — but never with such a sudden, youthful flame of loyalty as kindled within me that night. Perhaps, in later and more peaceful days, we have declined somewhat in zeal ; but I re-

member how in those dark and troublous times
the toast went with a thrill fit to stir a man in
his grave. I recall those occasions as clear as
a picture ; the ring of fine gentlemen, with
brimming glasses uplifted, a single fervent sentiment in their faces ; and I hear again the ring
of the shivered glass.

The Stuarts are this and that, and when all
is said, I do not know that I love the line over-
much ; but we have always followed the King,
whatsoever he might be. It is bred in the bone
of us ; we can do no otherwise.

III

A DEN OF THIEVES

IT must have been past midnight when we
quitted the Orle of Martlets and struck into
the road leading towards Grovely Wood, a
tract of forest lying about three miles to the
northward of Wilton. No sooner had we
reached the skirts of the wood than the Captain, quitting the road, plunged into its branchy
depths. Save for an occasional patch of star-
spangled sky above the bourgeoning tree-tops,
there seemed nothing to guide us, for the place
was pitch-black ; nevertheless, the Captain held
steadily onwards along some sort of rough
track.

" Ye have just seen the top-side of the King's
party, Mr. Langford," he remarked. " Now
y' are to behold the bottom. His Majesty's
business requires some singular instruments, and
its execution sometimes takes his servants into
strange places."

A Den of Thieves

As he spoke, there fell upon our ears a confused noise of shoutings, and, a few paces further, we descried a red glow, as of a great fire, behind the serried black trees.

"The clapper-dogeons are in their altitudes, as usual," observed the Captain. "For drinking, roaring drunk, hand-to-fist, and raising the Black Spy in general, commend me to the Mul-Sack's crew."

Before I had time to ask his meaning, we emerged upon a wide, irregular clearing, where stood a dark mass of building, which seemed to be a chapel. A most prodigious din was going on inside; the painted windows glowed upon the night, and a stream of light shone from the open doorway, through which we could see a fantastical crowd of men and women seated about long tables, feasting, gambling, and quarrelling. Two sentries, posted one on each side of the doorway, lay propped against the wall, sound asleep ; a pot of ale stood on one side of each, and on the other, his match smouldered in the grass. Planted in the ground, tipsily askew, in front of them, were their match-lock rests, while the ponderous weapons themselves

were leaned against the wall. The red ruins
of a huge fire, burning midway between the
chapel and the trees, dimly revealed the figures
of several horses picketed near by, and the outlines of some covered wagons beyond.

At the moment of our arrival there was a
sudden increase in the clamor, and the wild
figures of two men, twisted together and fighting like cats, appeared upon the orange patch
of the doorway, swayed to and fro, dropped
upon the sward outside, and lay there wrestling. Other figures thronged after them, and
in a moment the combatants were hidden from
view by a howling mob.

Captain Jacobus dismounted briskly, drew a
pistol from his holster, and strode into the
crowd, shouldering them to right and left.
" Mark ho!" some one shouted, and the cry
was caught up and repeated twice or thrice;
then, with a complete change of accent, " The
Captain! Way for the Captain!" Catching
his horse by the bridle, and following close
upon his heels, I came up to find the Captain
slashing the writhing gladiators on the ground
across the head and face with his heavy riding-

switch, and rating them the while like a couple of curs.

"Do I pay you to kill each other, you filthy scoundrels," he cried, as the bloody and dishevelled ruffians staggered stupidly to their feet. "No more of it, or I will have the skin flogged off you by inchmeal. Take the horses to stable, some of you. Come in, Mr. Langford;" and we stepped across the threshold.

The place was thronged with a crew of more villainous tatterdemalions than I had ever before clapped eye upon in one place, and the reek of the atmosphere caught my throat. Stuck upon the tables, and in iron wall sconces, there were enough candles burning to lighten a street; the unsightly reliques of a huge meal littered the trestle-tables that stood along the walls; and round them was gathered a horrible tribe of beggars and their callets. There was scarce a complete man amongst them; the most had lost a limb in the late wars, and the rest would lack an eye or an ear, or perhaps a nose; while as for those among their women who were not old, lean, and hag-like, the boldness of their manner of attire and behavior flushed the blood into my face. 39

Upon our right hand, almost midway in the
wall, an arch opened upon what had doubtless
been a private chapel, but was now a kitchen,
furnished with a great stone fireplace, about
which two or three stout wenches were busy
cooking. As we entered, the crowd, falling
suddenly silent, made way for us. Right in
front, upon the daïs where once had stood the
altar, an old man sat in a high-backed chair, at
a small table, dozing asleep as placid as though
he were alone in a wilderness. His face,
burnt dark by the weather, was evil and handsome, and his long white curls flowed upon his
shoulders. Immediately above him rose the
tall east window, wherein, through the smoke,
I dimly discerned the pale figure of our Lord.

At the jingle of our spurs upon the stones,
the ancient arose, and saluting, approached us.

"What the devil, Mul-Sack!" cried Captain Jacobus. "Do you keep order no better
than this? Had I been Captain Crook, with a
troop of dragoons at my back, you would have
been jogging to Tyburn in fetters now."

"Why, that's the truth, Captain, and
where's the use of denying it?" returned the

other, with a kind of cringing insolence. "The rogues are fit to make your heart ache, you know so well as I, Captain. If you please to enter your own room, Captain, the wenches will light a fire and bring the best we have."

"Quick about it," said the Captain, shortly, and turning his back upon the man Mul-Sack, and going to a door in the north wall, he took a key from his pocket and unlocked it.

Mul-Sack, crying out some commands in a strange language, plucked a score of candles from the wall and followed, when we found ourselves in a vaulted octagonal chamber, which must once have been the sacristy. Two or three of the wenches bustled in and out with fuel and dishes; in a few moments a fagot was blazing on the hearth, and a plentiful meal smoking on the table. The Captain unlocked a great chest that stood against the wall, and drew forth bottles of Xeres wine; and we fell to very heartily, Mul-Sack coming in and out the while, solicitous that we should lack nothing. When we had finished, the table was cleared swiftly, the door shut, and we were left alone. Captain Jacobus, who forgot nothing, dived once more into the chest, and placed upon the table paper and ink, pens and sealing-wax.

"Write what you have to write, and I'll despatch it forthwith," said he; and sitting down by the fire with his back to me, the Captain lit a long pipe.

I took my head in my hands and tried to think what I must write to Barbara. Clearly I must tell her the truth of the case, and leave her free to renounce me. 'T was the least and the most I could do: but I knew well enough she would not consent; and although there was consolation in the thought, how could I endure that her lot should be bound up with that of a broken man and an outlaw? True, the present conspiracy might succeed, the King come to his own again, and all be well; but I owned to myself I had small hopes of it. There are things in this world must be carried thorough-stitch in spite of one's teeth; here was one of them; every word I wrote, I thought of Barbara reading it, and when the letter was done there was no more virtue in me.

"To Salisbury? A decas there and a decas back," said the Captain, as I handed him the enclosure. "Have you a couple of crowns?"

I gave him the money, and he left the room, to return with Mul-Sack.

"The letter shall be delivered so soon as the city gates are opened," said the old gentleman. "I do not know your name, sir, but you seem a mighty proper young gentleman, and 't is a pleasure to serve you," he added politely.

"Sit down, Mul-Sack, help yourself to liquor, and get to business," said Captain Jacobus. "What of Mr. Armorer?"

"Trepanned. And the harmanbacks picqued to kumirle and lodged him in the King's Inn," returned the other.

The Captain, twisting his mustache, seemed to digest this intelligence, then he turned to me.

"He wishes to convey," he said, "that Mr. Nicholas Armorer, my lieutenant, has been captured by constables, carried to London, and confined in Newgate. Stow your whids and plant 'em," he added to Mul-Sack. "Tell us how it happened in the King's English."

"How should I know," said Mul-Sack,

coolly. "Mr. Armorer must have had a accident in filching the mails from Thurloe's express from Flanders, and afterwards fallen in with Crook or some of his gans; for, going out upon the night-sneak, we found the cold meat of Thurloe's rider Kaines with a sword-slash in his throat. We stripped him for what he was worth, which was cursed little, but found no screeves on him. So 't is a nice question whether Mr. Armorer destroyed the mails before he was taken, or whether the soldiers carried them to Thurloe. Aye, Nick Armorer's gone out on the boman hen once too often, Captain. Here's to his bilking the nubbing-cheat,[1] but I would n't lay a groat upon the chance," and the old robber tossed off a tot of French brandy and turned his glass upside-down upon the table.

The Captain sat ruminating gloomily for a space, Mul-Sack sipping his liquor the while, and casting sidelong glances out of his narrow eyes at his chief.

"And what of the brothers Dickenson?" inquired Captain Jacobus.

[1] Cheating the gallows.

A Den of Thieves

I learned afterwards the details of the auda-
cious plot to which this question referred : indeed (though not without qualms), I assisted later
in its development. There were two brothers
Dickenson, Mr. Emanuel and Mr. Jedediah,
both of whom were goldsmiths, — Mr. Emanuel
carrying on a great trade in Paul's Churchyard
in London, and Mr. Jedediah a solid business in
the High Street, Winchester. Mr. Emanuel
was a zealous member of the Rump, which
appeared to the Captain much more than a justi-
fication for robbing the pair. So he forged a
letter to Emanuel, purporting to be from the
wife of Jedediah, inviting Emanuel to her husband's funeral ; while Mul-Sack, who was a
person of grossly misused education, indited another, precisely similar, to Jedediah, on behalf of
Mrs. Emanuel. When the brothers were fairly
on their way to each other's obsequies, Mul-Sack
was to rob the Winchester shop, while Captain
Jacobus rifled the house in Paul's Churchyard.

"According to the time allowed," said Mul-
Sack in answer to the Captain's question, "the
letters would be delivered this morning, so that
both the fools should have started to-night. They

will be sure to travel at night, for fear of you and me, Captain."

"Why, 't is very well," said the Captain; "and what next?"

"No more that I wot of, save that Noll's upon the road to-morrow, travelling up from Winchester. I drink to his speedy damnation," said Mul-Sack.

The Captain appeared quite unmoved at this piece of news. "How many outriders?" he asked, knocking out the ashes of his pipe upon the palm of his hand.

"Seven."

"Ah?" said the Captain. "And now I'll bid you good-night; for these are ill hours, and we must be stirring betimes. And what think you of Mul-Sack, King of the Beggars, Mr. Langford?" he continued, when the old man had shut the door behind him.

I was dazed and bewildered with the staggering sequence of events, and tired as a dog; but I had somehow acquired an impression that Mul-Sack was a very villanous rascal, and I said so.

"Y' are right," said the Captain. "A most deadly varlet. But he is supple as a glove with me, and his vagabonds are my secret-service men from Southampton port to London town. John Thurloe thinks he owns a secret service, but mine is worth forty on 't. My pilgrims take what they can get, disobedience is sudden death, and, in the upshot, the King is very well served. Can ye sleep on straw, Mr. Langford? I know no softer bed ;" and the Captain flung himself on a huge truss of fresh straw that had been laid in readiness, rolled himself in his cloak, and seemed to sleep at once.

I laid myself down likewise, and in spite of sorrow, my weariness was so sore that I dropped straightway into the profound slumber of youth.

IV

ON THE ROAD

IT seemed that I had scarce closed my eyes,
when I was awakened by a rough shaking ;
and, sitting up, I gazed stupidly at the unfamiliar
chamber, grisly with the gray light of dawn which
filtered in at the narrow window.   For a moment
I knew not where I was : then my eyes encountered the Captain's, —who was lugging on his long
boots,—and the memory of my disasters came back
upon me at a blow.

"'T is boot-and-saddle, Mr. Langford, and
brisk about it," said the Captain.   "We have
six miles to ride to breakfast."

"I am ready," I answered shortly ; for I
felt exceeding sleepy, and not a little miserable.
I thought upon the waking that should have
been mine, the merry anticipations that were
wont to sit upon my pillow ; and I raged as I
saw myself torn from happiness, and compelled

to trot at the heels of this indefatigable conspirator. Captain Jacobus put away all his
effects, and set the room as neat as a parlor,
while I dragged on my boots and girt on sword
and pistols, — Manning's pistols. Then we
passed into the body of the chapel, the Captain
locking the door of the sacristy behind him.

The trestles had all been piled against the
wall, and the beggars lay huddled like swine
upon a thick bed of straw, deep in a drunken
slumber. Some were covered with sheep-skins,
some with foul old cloaks, while to others, who
lay in their rags, sleep gave a new and more
gross and filthy look than they wore awake.
The place was dim and ashy gray, but a lustrous
reflection from the lightening sky without shone
from the majestic figure in the eastern window
painted by forgotten monks, gazing serenely
down upon the sleeping thieves.

Outside, in the clear air, where brown and
ragged continents of cloud were sailing swiftly
across a sky as bright as a shield, I drew deep
breaths that renewed me like wine ; I began to
feel my own man again, and fit for the day's
work. The two sentries, awakened, I suppose,

by the nip of the morning, were playing at putt on the grass. The Captain despatched them to fetch the horses; and while they were gone we laved head and hands in a clear spring that bubbled up hard by. Mounting, we cleared the wood, and soon we saw the great pillars of Stonehenge heaved black against the sunrise. Leaving them on our left, we descended into the valley and crossed the Avon by the bridge at Amesbury, where we broke our fast and had the horses fed and groomed.

"And now," said the Captain, "let us consider where we stand, Mr. Langford. At present, Captain Crook hath the stronger cards, it appears. To confiscate the Langford estates, and to nab Nick Armorer, with or without old Thurloe's mails, is very well for one week's work; but it shall turn to his undoing, — as he might have said himself. Meanwhile, cut two more notches on his score. Now to Winchester to see how squares go with Brother Jedediah, and thence to Farnham, where we lie the night, if the horses can get there, and nothing delays us on the road."

During the silent ride from Grovely Wood I

had considered the situation; I had something to say upon it; and the sooner it was out the better.

"Captain Jacobus," I began, "you have taken the kindliest interest in my fortunes, although I have no guess why you should have done so; and I am loth to say what I must —"

I paused to grope for words, while the Captain surveyed me keenly.

"Speak out, Mr. Langford," he said; and I took heart and continued.

"Here am I slung into the King's service willy-nilly; and although I am ready enough to bear my part, you must permit me to distinguish. I will have no hand in your doings on the road, Captain. It doth not take my fancy, going out upon the pad."

"You would say, a gentleman should not do 't?" said the Captain, deliberately.

"I did not say so," I retorted rather angrily.

"Mr. Langford," he returned, "y' are young, and suffer under the sweet illusions proper to youth. You call yourself a King's man of discretionary years, and yet you do not appear to comprehend that the country is down under the bloody paws of usurpers and regicides, who possess no rights in law. Did we plunder Royalists, it would be different. But we do but take our own from those who robbed us thereof. A pox of your scruples! You appear to be curst with a right puritanical conscience, for the thing is as plain as a pike."

"Nevertheless, I will not do 't," I said.

"You will take your own way, then, as I shall take mine," said Captain Jacobus. "Your zeal of conscience does not extend to me, I presume?"

"Why, no," I answered, a little out of countenance, "your affairs are no business of mine."

"No? Had I made the same reflection last night, this notable debate might never have fallen between us. But let that pass. I am glad to hear it, too; for, to deal plainly with you, Mr. Langford, I do not allow young persons to interfere with my Christian liberty."

I had no more to say, and although I knew I was in the right, I did not feel so. In the pause that followed, the Captain called for the reckoning.

On the Road

"Do you travel upon your own charges?" he asked, with the imperturbable amenity of manner that was his constant characteristic. "I am sorry to trouble you, but 't is a question we must settle, for convenience' sake."

I searched my pockets; but I had given my last crown to pay the messenger who carried my letter to Barbara, and, with a very red face, I had to own as much.

"Why, no matter," cried the Captain. "His Majesty lets no man want, if he can help it. Take a few of the King's pistoles for present use," and he pressed upon me a handful of broad pieces. I had no resource but to pocket them, which I did with a strong reluctancy.

"Be not so bashful, man," said Jacobus. "What! 't is but a matter of business. Besides," he added dryly "there are plenty more where those came from."

I saw what he meant, of course, and straightway fell into a black temper. After denouncing highway robbery, I found myself condemned to live upon the proceeds thereof, — a doubly false position; for not only had I never earned them, but it seemed that in future I was to stand by and watch Captain Jacobus doing all the work and taking all the risk, and afterwards to share in the booty. I had yet to learn that a man may sometimes be thrust, against his will, into a false position, where no kicking against the pricks may serve him. So that after leaving the inn at Amesbury, I rode many miles in a sulky silence, — angry with myself, and cursing the Captain.

We travelled for the most part across country, over the noiseless, shining downs, a merry wind whistling past our ears, and a vasty cope of pale blue sky about us, until we came out above the ancient city of Winchester lying in the cup of a deep valley, intersected by a silver ribbon of running water. The town was four-square, enclosed within a great wall; in the midst rose the long back and the squat gray tower of the Cathedral, girt on all quarters with smaller towers and steeples, their vanes a sparkle of gold in the sunlight. The Captain drew rein and turned to me.

"Mr. Langford," said he, "the moment we set foot within yonder city our lives are in

Jeopardy, for though Royalist at heart, the place is ruled by the other side, since Noll beat down the castle in the name of his God. I am a known man, nor do I choose to disguise myself for a junto of prick-eared burgesses, and I am going to dine and to bait my horse at the George Inn. But if you have no stomach for needless dangers, Mr. Langford, there is no need for your mother's son to fly in the face of them. I have a hundred broad pieces in my saddle-bag. Take them and ride down to Southampton Water yonder, ship across to Flanders, join the Court at Cologne, and take your chance of a place about His Majesty. You will not starve, at any rate, whatever befall."

I looked at the keen-eyed, alert figure on the big red horse, but could make nothing of the blank vizard of his face.

"Do you want to be rid of me?" I asked.

"No," returned the Captain; and I believed him.

"Unless I sell my horse and go to work in the fields, and so quit the King's service, I must still exist upon your bounty, it appears," I said haltingly.

"Oh, hang your scrupulosity!" cried the Captain. "Have I not told you 't is His Majesty's wages? Am I not his paymaster? Are you his comptroller of taxes? Body o' me! Shalt say hast earned 'em before the week's out, I'll warrant ye. Come! Dine with me at the George, or take this bag of my namesakes and the part of discretion, ship yourself to Flanders, and be done with it."

"I will dine with you with all my heart, sir," says I.

"Well, and I thought you looked hungry," says the Captain, with a chuckle; and with that we paced forward down the hill.

We entered the city by the West-gate, beside which rose a huge pile of shattered masonry, the remains of the Black Tower which Cromwell, ten years before, had bombarded to make a breach into the Castle; and, "Noll is a very proper man, and the best soldier in England, with a maggot in his brain which keeps him o' the wrong side," quoth Jacobus, as we passed. The George is a pleasant house, half-way down the High Street, and the master tavern of the place. Captain Jacobus, who was as resolute to live upon the marrow of the land, when he was in funds, as he was contented to go pinched on bread and cheese when his Pactolus ran low, ordered a meal of the best. No healthy man can lack hope and a certain dash of happiness so long as he is well fed; and in spite of my troubles, I felt singularly at peace, with a noble dinner and a pint of generous wine inside me, as we lounged in the doorway giving upon the street.

And here I was aware of a stout-built, dignified, ill-humored-looking gentleman emerging from the throat of a narrow archway upon the opposite side, which led to the Cathedral Close. There was some strong, indefinable quality about the man which held my attention, and I watched him with a lazy interest in his approach. He had a proud, red face, little steely blue eyes under massy brows, and locks of ash-gray hair curling on his shoulders; and was habited in a plain dark suit of cloth of a puritanical cut, with a broad falling lace collar and cuffs. He made towards us, and had his foot upon the steps, when the Captain, who was leaning against the opposite door-post

smoking a cigarro, suddenly caught sight of
him. I have never seen so quick and shocking
a change in a man's face as passed upon the
Captain's at that moment. He went dark red,
his eyes enlarged, the veins in his forehead
swelled, his mustachios bristled, and he stiffened all over. The puritanical gentleman with
the great nose regarded us both with a keen,
frowning glance as he mounted the steps. Now
the doorway was not very wide, and there was
scant room for a third person to pass; so that
I drew back slightly, expecting the Captain to
do likewise. But had his feet been socketed in
the floor, Jacobus could not have stood more
unremoved. The stranger, in consequence,
brushed heavily against him in passing, but
went on without a word of apology or so much
as a look. The Captain's eyes followed him,
much as a leashed terrier stares at a rat, until
he had disappeared within.

"What the devil is the matter?" I said.
"Who is that?"

But Jacobus did not hear me.

"Now if it were not for that same gentility
you prate so much about," said he, "I could

HE REGARDED US WITH A KEEN, FROWNING GLANCE.

have dirked the man as he passed. The Lord
Protector would have been dead on that door-
step, and England herself again. Well, you
see I have not done it; and by God, I think I
am a fool!"

"The Lord Protector Cromwell?" I cried
in amaze.

"Did you not know him? You will, be-
fore all 's done. And now I think 't is full time
we took the road, Anthony,"— for the Captain
had taken to using me with this friendly familiarity since our little conversation on the hill.
"Pay you the reckoning, while I see to the
nags," and he disappeared toward the stables.

As we clattered down the High Street, Captain Jacobus, who had explained to me the
nature of his designs upon the brothers Dickenson, called my eyes to a large shop at the corner,
where the memorial cross now stands that was
set up some ten years later, in the time of the
great Pestilence. The shutters were up, and I
read upon a handsome swinging sign the legend,
"Jedediah Dickenson, Jeweller and Goldsmith."

"All snug for Mul-Sack," remarked the
Captain.

Captain Jacobus

"Well, you sail near the wind," I said.

"To a superficial person. But I give you credit for a better discernment. The King's taxes must be collected somehow."

We left the town by the East-gate, skirted Saint Giles's hill, and came out upon the Alresford road, which goes rising and falling with the bare downs. The sight of Alresford battlefield brought my father's death sharply to remembrance; and it struck me as highly probable that his son was riding to a like fate in the same insensate quarrel. A little after we came in sight of Chilton Candover, a tiny village at the junction of the road we were now upon with the main road from Winchester to Reading, which runs direct through Kingsworthy instead of winding about through Alresford. I was beginning to wonder why we had fetched a compass, when I espied in front of us, upon the Kingsworthy road, a coach and pair, followed by a knot of outriders, the sun sparkling upon their steel caps and accoutrements. I glanced at the Captain, who was staring fixedly at the swiftly moving party. He turned his head, and our eyes met.

60

On the Road

"Anthony," he said abruptly, "that is the Protector's coach, and I am going to stop it. What are you going to do?"

"Under the circumstances, I am coming with you. There are one, two — seven outriders, and Oliver is not the man to go weaponless himself."

"Ah, but I have his pistols," said Jacobus, pointing to a brace of petronels strapped to his holsters, which he must have taken from the coach in the stableyard of the George. "There is an alehouse in Chilton Candover, and if the guard stops to drink, why, I hold the brewer's life in the hollow of my hand."

The low sun shone full into Jacobus's face as he turned towards me in his saddle: his hat was pulled over his eyes, but I could see the muscles of his mouth twitching the while I hesitated. A vision of all that the Protector's death would mean flashed through my mind. It meant Barbara to me, and vengeance of my father's death. For the rest, the King with his own, the Cavaliers restored, England free. Was not the regicide's life already forfeit on a hundred counts? And a thirst for the blood

61

of that grayhaired, brazen-bowelled rebel in the gilded coach yonder burned within me. I glanced after it, and, sure enough, it was crawling unattended up the hill beyond the village. Then, of a sudden (it sounds a simple thing to say), I saw myself explaining the matter to Barbara, and beheld the look upon her listening face. It could not be done.

"We cannot shoot a defenceless man, Captain," I said steadily.

To this day I do not know what Captain Jacobus had originally intended : perhaps he had not made up his mind, and merely took the brace of pistols while he had the chance ; for scarce were the words out of my mouth, when he struck spurs into his horse, leaped the low hedge at the side of the road, and set off at full gallop in a straight line for the Lord Protector's coach. I followed him upon the instant, and after cutting off a corner, we came out upon the road again as the coach vanished round a bend between steep banks. Glancing over my shoulder, I caught a glimpse of the group of soldiers clustered about the ale-house, scarce a quarter-mile behind. The Captain executed what was doubtless a very familiar manœuvre. With a cocked pistol in each hand, guiding his horse with his knees, he rode up alongside the coachman, crying, "Stand!" in a great voice. The startled driver pulled his horses upon their haunches. At the same instant a shrill whistle sounded, and the Protector thrust forth head and shoulders, a silver whistle in his teeth.

"Ye insolent rogues," said he, in a thick, choleric voice, "what would ye have?"

A sudden, boyish impulse took me. "Justice!" I cried. "You have the name of a just man, my Lord Cromwell. Why am I, Anthony Langford, of Langford Manor, that never lifted a finger against the laws, driven out of house and home by a troop of your soldiers?"

The heavy eyebrows came down over the small sparkling eyes, and the Lord Protector glared at me, then past me at Jacobus.

"What, Langford of the Plymouth plot! y' are well met. I have heard of you from Mr. Thurloe. And who are you, sir, with the pistols?"

"Damn you, out of the way, man!" shouted Jacobus, passionately, wrenching at my bridle. I do not know what he would have done, for at that moment a mighty clatter of hoofs broke upon our ears, and the whole body of outriders came swerving round the corner at full gallop, not fifty paces behind us.

"Too late," cried the Captain. "Come away!" and striking spurs into his horse, he dashed off down the road, and I after him, the dragoons thundering at our heels. We heard a hoarse shout of command, and the soldadoes roaring out a summons to surrender: then the explosion of a pistol, and the scream of a bullet over our heads. At that the Captain turned his horse, and we leaped the hedge as two more shots sang past us. A fourth struck my nag on the withers, but did no great harm, for by that time we had got well ahead. The ground was smooth and undulating grass-land, and for a long while we kept neck to neck, and the men behind us in a compact body, until we crossed a soft place, after which our pursuers began to straggle somewhat. Then up hill and down dale, mile after mile, we rode headlong, hoping fervently that the breeding of the horses would carry us through until the night fell. Already the sun was dipping below the rim of the hills ; we rode in a colored twilight ; and looking back as we topped a rise, I could see but four riders, a mile or so behind.

But I was a heavy man, and as we breasted the next hill I felt my nag beginning to fail. Still we held on without slackening, until the figures of our pursuers had become mere blurs in the gathering dusk. Suddenly my horse stumbled, recovered, stumbled again, pitched forward so that I had but just time to save myself, and lay still, the blood pouring from his nostrils. The Captain pulled up.

"His heart's broke. Mount behind me," he said.

"I can run," I replied, and with my arm across his crupper we set off again at a vengeance of a pace. We had gone about three miles, I suppose, when I felt the horse give under me, and had but just time to cry a warning before he came heavily to the ground. The Captain was thrown, but got to his feet immediately. The poor beast struggled upon its fore-feet with wild eyes, but fell back again with a groan. The Captain peered into the darkness, then laid his ear to the ground. There was no more sign of pursuit.

"I'll risk it," he said, and drawing a pistol, he shot the animal through the head. Then he took off the saddle and bridle, shouldered them, and we marched towards a wood that loomed darkly near by. Once within the shelter of the trees, we flung ourselves down, utterly exhausted.

V

ON THE ROAD — THE INN AT FARNHAM

AFTER a while the Captain roused himself and sat up. "The next point is, where are we?" says he, and strolls towards the borders of the wood. I dragged myself to my feet and followed him. As the trees grew more thinly, the ground began upon a sharp descent into a valley, where some lights twinkled, and over against us, on the brow of the opposite hill, we could discern in the steely light of the stars the dim outlines of a range of great buildings.

"Well, we have reached our bourne in spite of Noll's dragoons," said Jacobus. "It is what I steered for, and Providence hath been kind. Here are we in the skirts of Holt Forest : there is Farnham Castle opposite, and supper stays for us in the vale, at the sign of the Smiling Lion. We must tramp it, my son."

So saying, we began to pick our way down the hill-side, — the Captain, although I offered to relieve him, with his harness on his back, — and soon struck upon the high-road. A couple of miles of weary trudging brought us upon the long main street of Farnham, when a horseman, whom we had heard trotting behind, coming level with us, pulled his horse into a walk, and paced slowly past us. Captain Jacobus peered keenly at him, edging nearer to get a better look. Then he dropped back a pace or two. "Jedediah Dickenson, as I live by bread!" he whispered. About a bow-shoot further on, a good-sized inn stood a piece back from the road, ruddy light bursting from the crevices of the shutters and streaming from the open door. Standing squarely in the doorway, at the top of a little wide flight of steps, a tall man with a gray beard was looking forth upon the night. No sooner had the Captain caught sight of this sombre figure than he clutched my arm.

"And Brother Emanuel too," he exclaimed with an oath.

A moment later the horseman in front of us stopped as though he had been shot, and bent limply

over his saddle-bow. Jacobus is a quick man by
nature and habit; but never did I see him act
more swiftly.

"Take Jedediah's bridle, turn the nag, and
lead him forward," he whispered. "Quick,
now!"

If ever there was a frightened man in this
world it was the Winchester goldsmith. I
caught a glimpse of his face as I passed. The
white of his skin above his fringe of beard shone
upon the darkness like a linen mask: he had
dropped his reins, and with both hands gripping
his saddle-bow, he was staring fixedly at the
graybeard in the doorway. I whipped the horse
round, and had much ado to hold him, for Captain Jacobus leapt up suddenly behind the saddle,
and crooked his arm about the traveller's throat.

"Steady, now," I heard him say to his victim,
as I led forward at a brisk walk. "Y' are safe
if you do not struggle: resist, and y' are a dead
man."

Save for the lights within the houses, the
street was perfectly dark; there was no one
abroad at that late hour, and we gained the
outskirts of the village unperceived. All at

once it occurred to me that, after all my fine
speeches, here was I art and part in a common
piece of toby work, and that for the second
time in one day. Upon the first occasion
there seemed nothing else to be done, and we
had paid dearly for 't. Now I had been be-
trayed by sheer inadvertence, in the hurry of the
moment. I stopped the horse and turned round.
The wretched Jedediah was still holding to the
pommel of his saddle, Jacobus, who seemed to
be kneeling on the crupper, still embraced his
neck, and I could dimly catch the outline of
the Captain's long nose and mustache over his
shoulder in the gloom.

"Captain," I said, "this is not in the
bond."

"In the King's name!" returned the Captain, like the snapping of a pistol. "Obey
orders, sir!"

I had not foreseen this, and there seemed no
answer to it, for Captain Jacobus undoubtedly
held his Majesty's commission, while I was a
sworn volunteer. I resumed my march, therefore, not without a sneaking satisfaction, for conscience was silenced within, and besides, 't was

excellent sport. After about a quarter of an hour of walk, the Captain, who appeared to have become mighty military all of a sudden, cried out to me to halt. Jumping off, he ordered Mr. Jedediah to dismount, which the goldsmith did without a word, in a somewhat dazed and fumbling fashion. Then acting under the Captain's brief commands, after tying the horse to the hedge, I took one arm while he took the other, and we squired our Bale-o'-grace across a field towards a barn that loomed in the darkness. Here the Captain stood over him with a pistol while I untied his garters (which were scarfs of black silk, of a richness quite unbefitting his station), wherewith we secured his wrists and ankles. Then we carried him into the barn, which was black-dark and smelled of hay and rats, until we stumbled over a truss and dropped him.

"I wish you a good-night, Mr. Dickenson," said the Captain, speaking into the darkness, "and a pleasant walk to Winchester, where, if all I have heard be true, y' are sadly wanted;" and with that we left him, latching to the great door behind us.

Captain Jacobus

"That was a close throw," the Captain said, as we retraced our steps. "Had it not been for the little accident with Oliver, I should have stopped one or other of them (by your good leave) before they could have met. However, all's well, notwithstanding."

"And what will come to Mr. Jedediah?" I asked.

"How should I know? He may die and go to the place appointed to his fellowship, or he may live and go to Winchester. But I'll wager he does n't set foot in Farnham to-night, and that's enough for me."

The Captain would have me ride the nag, and in this wise we regained the village, where, after picking up the saddle, I rode into the stable-yard at the sign of the Smiling Lion, while Jacobus went within to order supper.

Upon crossing the threshold of the inn some minutes later, after having seen the horse properly cared for, I was stricken to hear the tones of a strong voice, as of a man preaching, issuing from the common room, instead of the droning rustical songs customary in such places. Pushing open the door I walked in. The long, low

room was bright with fire and candle ; three or
four country-fellows stood about the great ingle,
long pipes in their hands, with blank, amazed
faces all turned towards the man who, from behind a jack of ale at the head of the table, was
speaking with a stern vehemence. In the great,
square-shouldered figure with the shaven upper
lip and the gray beard I recognized Mr. Emanuel Dickenson, whom we had seen but now in
the doorway, and whom his brother Jedediah
had taken for his ghost. Jacobus was sitting
sideways on the edge of the table, with his hat
set awry, swinging a leg, and staring with a
very malapert air at the lecturer, who appeared
to be addressing him directly.

"Art thou a damned heretic or a popish
dog ?" he was crying, as I entered. "Y' are
a whiffling, trumpery fop, by any way of thinking. What make you, disturbing honest men
at their meat in their inn, with your lewd conversation ? I know ye, who you are. Y' are
one of those sons of Belial, those notorious, outrageous evil livers, the back-stairs gentlemen of
the bloody Stuart, who range up and down the
country like Satan scouting for a prey, disorder-

ing God's chosen with your abominable offences. It is insufferable. It is not to be borne. The Lord Protector shall take order upon it. Ye shall hang in chains on Newmarket Heath, my ruffling cavalier canary bird. Mark me —"

"I will," said Jacobus. "Ye . . . . !" The Captain delivered himself of a single unsurpassable sentence, which cannot be written here, referring to the Parliament of which Emanuel was a member, and, leaning forward, dealt the Puritan a rattling buffet on the mouth. A hoarse shout went up from the bystanders as the big man leaped to his feet and began lugging at his rapier. But the Captain was too quick for him. Springing back as nimbly as a goat, he set his shoulder against the end of the table, and seeing what he would be at, I sprang to his side. We ran the long board upon Emanuel like a battering-ram, pinning him against the wall. The edge caught him in the wind, I suppose, as he stumbled back, for he doubled up and fell upon his face among the dirty platters with a mighty crash. At that moment the landlady, a huge woman with a scarlet face, came running in, and comprehending the state of affairs at a glance, made, open-mouthed, at Jacobus and me.

"Out with you!" she shouted. "Out with you! I will have none of your roaring bullies of Cavaliers in my house. Out, I say!"

Pressed by this formidable virago, who continued to revile us at the top of her pipe, we had no choice but to retreat, and so backed into the hall. My hopes of supper had begun to dwindle dismally, and even Jacobus seemed out-faced for once, when there fell a sudden diversion.

"Why, what is the matter?" cried a voice from the stairway.

We all turned round, and there, standing at the lighted stair-foot, was a bright spring beauty of a wench, with a great coronal of red hair; and methought she looked at us very kindly. The landlady turned obsequious in a twinkling, after the manner of her kind.

"Why, no great matter, Mistress Curle," she began. "'Tis a shame that you should be so put upon. But these Cavalier gentlemen —"

"Oh, sirs, are you for his Majesty?" cried the girl with sparkling eyes.

Jacobus rose to the occasion, while I was thinking about it : he stepped forward, removing his hat and bowing low.

"Poor servants of the King we are, at your service, Madam, for I perceive you cannot but be for God and the Cause. We have been upon his Majesty's business all day — I care not who hears me — I say, upon the King his service, with neither bite nor sup; and now we are to be flung into the road, it appears, to make room for a bloody regicide."

The landlady began a voluble explanation, but the girl broke in on it and silenced her.

"Gentlemen," said she, "if y' are the King's friends y' are mine also, and it will pleasure Mrs. Beatrice Young and myself greatly if you will sup with us above stairs. We shall expect you in a few minutes."

So saying, she curtseyed, and turned to go up stairs, carrying the baffled hostess with her. Meanwhile the idlers in the common room had crowded to listen. The Captain suddenly drew a pistol and levelled it.

"Back, you vermin!" he said, making a step forward; and the men hustled back into the room like sheep, falling over one another. They slammed to the door, and we could hear them bolting it.

"Now, if Emanuel has any stomach left for a fight (which I misdoubt me) they will stay his eviting the room for fear of me without," remarked the Captain. "Let us go make a toilet."

A house-wench showed us to a room, where we did our best to remove the dust and the blood-stains of the day's work.

"Why, what a thing it is," observed Jacobus, surveying me when we were ready, "to go about with a guileless, innocent, boyish face like yours, my son! For all the years I've been upon the road, never till now have I been bid to supper by a lady of any reputation."

We found Mistress Curle and her companion, a short, black-eyed, ruddy young lady, with a saucy bit of a nose, in a panelled chamber where a brisk fire burned on the hearth and a plentiful meal was smoking on the table.

"My cousin, Mrs. Beatrice Young," said Mistress Curle, leading the dark young lady forward. "Since I have no one to present me, I

must e'en do the office for myself. Mrs. Mariabellah Curle, gentlemen," said she, curtseying.

"This is my friend, Mr. Anthony Langford,
of Langford Manor; and my name is—" said
the Captain, bowing—"is Jacobus, of the
King's Highway."

"And are you the great Captain Jacobus,"
exclaimed Mrs. Mariabellah, "who stopped my
father's coach after his deprivation by the Roundheads, and gave him a bag of broad-pieces?
Oh, this is better and better!"

"And are you then the daughter of Bishop
Curle of Winchester?" asked Jacobus.

"The very same," cried she; "and Mrs.
Beatrice here is daughter to the Dean. But
come, let us fall to with the appetite befitting
those of the good party. Why," continued this
lively young woman, when we had sat down,
"had it not been for you, Captain, we two
should never have dared to take the road with
none but a little foot-page to guard us. But we
knew you kept the highway and would endure
no rivals; and, indeed, we hoped to meet you,
for after all the stories we have heard in our
sleepy, quiet little village, you cannot think how

I have longed to behold a real Cavalier ! And a highwayman, too ! Oh, brave ! A glass of wine with you, Captain, and with you, sir."

And she drank to us both, one after the other, with the prettiest grace imaginable ; and demure Mrs. Beatrice, blushing and twinkling, followed the lead she set.

The ladies made us extraordinary good cheer, seasoning it with fine courtly speeches ; but as for me, I was so deadly famished, that, with the best will in the world, I could scarce find fitting answers : my wits drowsed, and even the Captain's tongue lagged somewhat. You are to remember we had been some fifteen hours in the saddle, and in the time had each of us ridden a horse to death, besides enduring other fatiguing adventures. I think that Mrs. Mariabellah must have perceived our condition, for she presently took the whole burden of talk upon herself, entertaining us with the story of her father the Bishop's misfortune, when the Parliament ousted him from his see in the year 1646, so that he must retire to his sister's house at the tiny hamlet of Soberton, where he died a year or so later. And Mrs. Beatrice's father, the Dean, had a similar history; for when Ironsides marched into Winchester with his New Model at his back, the head of the Cathedral was forced to beat a swift retreat to his living at Over Wallop. But even thence Puritan malice pursued him, for Cromwell, hot from the sack of Basing House, descended upon Over Wallop, plundered the ill-starred old gentleman of his chief possessions, and set a scab of an Independent tinker over his head.

"So you will understand we bear no love to the powers that be," cried Mrs. Mariabellah. "I would even love to behold an English Barthol-omew-Massacre. There have we been for years and years and years, cooped up in the country, see-ing no one, hearing nothing, living a life so deadly dull I marvel the beasts of the field can suffer it. At last I said we would take advantage of an old pledge and go visit my father's brother at Guild-ford, and see something of life if we could before we were old and ugly, let me die if I would not! So here we are, you see."

"I make you my compliments," said the Captain. "I drink your health in a bumper, Madam, and yours, Mrs. Beatrice. Fill up, Anthony."

When at length the cloth was drawn, and the rich hues of burnt claret glowed in the mahogany, " Prithee," said Mrs. Mariabellah, " tell us of adventures." So, turn about, we told the tale of that day's exploits ; and I vow I would have undergone our toils and perils twice over to gain such a pretty pair of listeners. The wine was heady and exhilarating, the audience rarely quickening to the intellectuals ; and although I have forgotten every word we said, I am persuaded that we magnified each other's deeds to most heroical proportions, and that we shone like demi-gods in the eyes of those two innocent and enraptured maidens.

" And so you have only one horse between you. Oh, what an iniquity !" cried Mrs. Mariabellah, when we were done with our tale.

" Well, I dare say we shall not go wanting one long," remarked the Captain.

" You shall not indeed," said Mrs. Beatrice. " Why, how lucky, Mary, that we brought a led horse in case of accident. He is yours from this moment, Captain. Take him for the King !"

The Captain rose and made a very grand bow. " Madam," he replied, " y' are too generous ;

Captain Jacobus

I cannot accept such a gift. But an if you can spare the nag, I will buy him very gratefully for the King, for his Majesty's business is pressing."

But the ladies would not hear of it ; and so we argued the matter back and forth.

"Just because we are women," said Mrs. Mariabellah, "we are not allowed to do aught for the King, forsooth ! "

"Why, very well," said Jacobus. "If you will not sell, and the King's noblesse forbids him to accept, we can but decide the issue by the cards. I will stake my horse against yours, at hazard, primero, quinze, all-fours, or what you will."

The maidens agreed, and calling for a new pack, down we sat to hazard. The end of it was, the Captain won ; and thus he got his occasion for a speech, the hope of which I knew very well had been at the bottom of his finicking.

"Ladies," said he, "you have this night done the King, aye, and the nation, a service perhaps greater than you know. 'T is not the first time the issues of a kingdom have turned upon a lady's gift. Be assured, his Majesty shall hear of it."

On the Road — Inn at Farnham

The Royalist ladies flushed bright for sheer pleasure ; and the scene, along with many another, remains upon my memory, nor will dislimn with time. There is the ruddy light shining and flickering upon the black panelling ; there is the glowing wine and the litter of painted cards ; with the two gay and beautiful girls in their fine glistering attire, curtseying side by side, with a grace that is half mockery and half earnest, to the Captain, who, a good deal flushed, with one hand at his heart, stands making a low-leg like a courtier.

VI

ON THE ROAD — THE GOLDEN FARMER

IT was late the next morning ere we awoke, although we had laid our plans to start at sunrise and to escort the two ladies so far as Guildford. When we came downstairs the land-lady (a changed and gracious being) informed us that they were already gone near half an hour. Mr. Dickenson, she added, had departed over night, "holding a bloody clout to 's jaw."

"We will breakfast at Guildford, Anthony," said Jacobus.

I had to agree with a good grace, though I disliked exceedingly this custom the Captain had of always breaking his fast some ten miles farther on ; it was nothing but sheer, senseless, superfluous energy on his part, a mere lust for factitious virtue. We found the horse the Captain had won, in the stable next our own

nag, — or rather Mr. Jedediah's, — a big-boned
gray gelding, a very serviceable beast. A lock
of his mane was knotted with scarlet ribbon.
I untied this ladies' favor, and a slip of paper
fell out, upon which these words were written
in a fair hand : —

"Ladies-errant seek other-guess heroes
Than laggardly, slug-a-bed Cavalieros."

I tossed the script to the Captain.

"What! a love-letter so soon!" said he.
"Very pretty," he added, reading it. "But
wait till they 're stopped by some scoundrel
foot-pad out upon the shark, and they 'll pipe to
a different tune, I 'll warrant ; for they 're outside my policies now."

I mounted the gray, and the Captain the
goldsmith's bayard, and we rode slowly up the
long slope to the ridge of the Hog's Back, along
which the road runs straight as a pike the whole
ten miles from Farnham to Guildford, bordered
on either side by a wide strip of velvet turf, and
enclosed with tall, luxuriant hedges. The east
wind had changed during the night, and an
odorous western gale blew at our backs, driving

great armadas of gray cloud overhead, whose shadows swept across the fair plains lying below, seen as we cantered along the wet grass through gaps in the flitting hedgerows; now and again a plump of rain would fall, like a shower of needles in the glints of sunshine. We had been riding thus for half an hour, perhaps, when we came in sight of a black dot where the lines of the road ran into the sky.

"There they are," said the Captain; and, setting spurs to our horses, we presently made out that the group was standing still, and consisted of four persons upon horseback, two of whom were ladies, and the third their groom; but who was the fourth?

"The laggards will be in time yet," said Jacobus, urging his horse to its utmost speed. As we drew nearer, I observed that the stranger, whose back was towards us, appeared to be delivering a speech; I could see the sparkle where the sun struck the pistol in his right hand as he gesticulated. I suppose Mrs. Mariabellah and Mrs. Beatrice found his eloquence something tedious, for, seeing our approach, they uttered a cry of delight and waved their kerchiefs; but the speaker merely glanced over his shoulder and went on with his oration.

"'T is the Golden Farmer, as God's-my-life!" cried the Captain, pulling his horse into a walk. "We must hear him out, Anthony, for unless you shoot him dead, there's no stopping him. The man talks like a mill-race, or a whole college of doctors. He would perish else. He only robs because it gives him such singular good opportunities of compelling an audience."

The orator was a burly, great-headed, gray-haired man with thick lips; half his face was hidden by a black mask, behind which his yellow eyes rolled as he harangued; the ladies and the lacquey, under the awe of his pistol, were ranged in front of him, like children before a schoolmaster.

"Hark you! are ye not mad toads, to use such arguments to me? I know your sex too well, Madam, to suffer myself to be prevailed upon by any painted Mrs. Bitchington among ye," shouted the Golden Farmer, in what appeared to be a peroration. "What talk of the King to me! Give me leave to tell ye, madonnas, that

87

I am king here, and that I have a household to support at the public charges as well as his Majesty. I collect my dues from all that pass, and why should you, who would fling away all your rhino upon mirrors, apricoke paste, French essences, and such like vain trifles, rob an honest freebooter upon his lawful occasions ? No, no, you jades ; this haughty spirit, this hyperbolical cant, this sham poverty, will not serve you here. A plague on you ! Untie your purse-strings quickly, or else I shall send you from the land of the living. Do you think I have no other-guess customers, that you keep me waiting upon you all the morning ?" concluded this outrageous ruffian, levelling his pistol.

The ladies cried out. My gorge rose at the man's vile insolence ; and I closed in upon him on the one flank, pistol in hand, and caught his wrist, as the Captain did the same on the other.

"I have never heard you speak better," said Jacobus. "But upon this occasion there will be no contributions."

"Curse you !" shouted the Golden Farmer, struggling, "what do you here ?"

"Bing avast, my bene-cove, bing avast," returned the Captain, using the thieves' lingo. "I bit the blow in the darkmans, and the doxies are my booty."[1]

"Tip me my snack, or I'll whiddle,"[2] cried the other.

"Not a doit. Give me your word to picque peaceably, or, by God, you go below for orders!" and the Captain put his pistol to the Golden Farmer's head.

"I'll picque, 't is all boman,"[3] said the freebooter, sullenly; whereupon we released him, and without another word, striking spurs into his horse, he wheeled and rode away.

"There goes a very dangerous companion," remarked Jacobus. "And y' are the first congregation that ever listened to his silver discourses without paying for the treat in gold."

He put his horse in motion, and we began to ride forward, four abreast, the white-faced little lacquey falling behind.

---

[1] "Be off, my friend, be off. I robbed the girls last night, and the booty is mine."

[2] "Give me my share, or I will inform upon you."

[3] "I'll go, 't is all square."

"We are infinitely beholden to you, gentlemen," cried Mrs. Mariabellah, who appeared somewhat changed and pale in the morning light, methought, while Mrs. Beatrice, though rosy as ever, wore a scared look about her dark eyes.

"We have a thousand apologies to make, on our part, for our laggard appearance," I said.

"Had I conceived of such a possibility," said the Captain, "I would never have gone to bed."

"And I should never have got up," said Mrs. Beatrice.

"Pardon me," returned Jacobus, "your fair cousin would have compelled you, for I know she had sworn to prove the force of her bright eyes upon an armed desperado."

"Y' are impertinent, sir," said Mistress Curle, reddening.

"Is 't not the truth, then, Madam? I am no courtier; I cannot embroider my sayings; I speak but for your welfare. Did you not say to yourself, or even, perhaps, to prudent Mrs. Beatrice, here, 'Now let us adventure, and see if one of these self-same robbers of the road will out-face a pretty damsel!' and therewithal you slip off like a couple of convent school-girls, whilst two poor gentlemen are trying to get a little piece of rest from the arduous fatigues incident to his Majesty's service. 'T was scarce kind, I think. Moreover, you run the risks of dangers you know nothing of. No, no, Madam, you cannot play Una without the Lion, in these tristful days," concluded the Captain, with an obvious relish.

I cursed Jacobus in my heart, for Mrs. Beatrice shot an appealing glance at me, and I could see that both girls were over-wrought and trembling from stress of the danger they had just escaped. They spurred a little in advance of us; and thus the Captain, plucking at his mustache according to his habit when disturbed in mind, fell into step side by side with me.

" *Fay ce que voudras* is a privilege at all times to be reserved for ladies, Captain," I remarked sufficiently loud for them to hear.

He looked at me doubtfully, then his face cleared. Jacobus was one of those natural philosophers whose ignorance of women embodies itself in a single simple theorem; and hence, in his relations with ladies, he frequently walked upon the brink of catastrophes wherefrom not even his excellent intentions could always save him.

" Why, 't is very well said, Anthony," he returned cheerily. " And if a man be permitted to stave off evil consequence, 't is all he can expect; he may sing *Nunc dimittis* upon it, and go his way."

We rode along in silence ; and gazing at the two graceful figures in front, moving to beat of hoofs through the blowing, changeful, shining landscape, I marvelled to find myself as cold as though I were before a picture. A year ago or thereabouts I would have played the lover, or at least dallied somewhat with the part ; now my mind reached back with a strong recoil to a blue-eyed damsel sitting lonely in a gray city leagues behind us, and I found that I cared not the toss of a coin whether or no I was ever to see those two pretty ladies again. When they were come to the top of the long hill that descends upon the tail of Guildford town they turned to await us, the wind fluttering their gay riding-dresses, and playing daintily with strayling locks.

The cloud was quite dispelled from a pair of flushed and kindly faces.

"Gentlemen," said Mrs. Mariabellah, "'t is very sad, but I think it will be proper for us to part here, though not, let us ever hope for always. How can we thank you for your valor?"

While she was speaking, the Captain had taken a couple of Jacobuses from his pocket; holding them on his saddle-bow he graved something upon each with the point of his dagger. He had been making of a little speech, and arranging a situation, as we came along, I could see, and now his time had come.

"Alas," said he, "'t is ever the way of this floating world that we cannot be where we would: sometimes we are fast a-bed when we should be in the saddle; and again, the King his service haleth us willy-nilly from delight. But since so it must be, set the crown upon your favorable kindness, I beseech you, ladies, and accept a token that should safe-guard you upon all the West Country roads, until the King comes home." And with his best air, dismounting, he gave a broad-piece to each lady, kissing, as he did so, the hand she stretched forth to receive it.

"And when that day comes, as it will swiftly, I vow there will be no more gallant gentleman, no, not even the King his Majesty, restored to place and honor, than Captain Jacobus," cried Mrs. Mariabellah.

I was standing at Mrs. Beatrice's knee; and thinking, I suppose, that I might feel a little cast into the shadow by the Captain's glittering performances, she glanced at me with a sudden kindly look. I thought it mighty pretty of the maiden, and I took her hand and saluted her.

"Madam," I said, "I pray you remember always I am your faithful and willing friend to serve you."

"And you, Mr. Langford," said she, "y' have gained two friends. Forget it not."

I made my adieux to Mrs. Mariabellah, who spoke with equal courtesy; but I could see her mind was possessed by Jacobus. Then the two ladies turned and rode away down the hill, followed by the little groom, to whom the Captain tossed a crown. We stood watching the lessening figures until they came to a turn in the road, when they looked back and flashed a kerchief in the sunshine.

"Youthful and fair and ignorant and good, — upon what a singular world those perilous eyes look out!" quoth the Captain, as we remounted. "I marvel what it must be like, Anthony. Well, your fair lady is a pretty toy, indeed. I bless God for her! But she is a sad hindrance to business; and I shall eat the bigger breakfast that we are no longer cumbered."

I knew better than to say what I thought, and we pursued our way in silence into the old steep town of Guildford, where we put up at the White Hart. When we were fairly on the road again, I reflected that there were thirty profitable miles of road to London, and plainly foresaw further difficulties with my pragmatical conscience. But although now and again big, ruddy, well-liking farmers would be jogging to meet us, or a coach with outriders would lumber by, Jacobus rode all day as peaceably as he had been a simple citizen. The dusk was gathering, and the broad river glassed a red sunset as we passed the Lord Protector's palace of Hampton Court, and the dark had fallen by the time we were climbing the hill to Putney Heath. The wind, which had been waxing steadily all day, roared in the thickets through which the road ascended, and the battered crescent of the moon in wane shone in flying gleams between serried and swiftly marching regiments of cloud. In one of these flashes I saw a horseman spurring past us, wrapped in a great furred cloak. A moment afterwards I heard the Captain's voice above the wind and the thrashing of the branches, shouting in my ear.

"I think your nag hath cast a shoe. See to 't before we go farther."

I dismounted instantly, and felt the beast's feet, to find him securely shod. As I raised myself to climb into the saddle again, there came another gleam of moonlight, and I glanced about for the Captain. A bow's shoot further along the road I saw two black figures motionless amid the tossing silver landscape ; Jacobus stood with levelled pistol, while the rider in the furred cloak seemed to be groping in his saddle-bags ; and beyond, a man hanged high upon a gibbet swang limply to and fro, chin to breast and toes to earth. Down the wind came an odious, heart-heaving waft, and a clinking of chains. The night shut

close again like a curtain : after discreetly waiting
a few moments, I rode slowly forwards ; and
presently discovered the Captain at my side. We
exchanged no word until we had passed beneath
the dead man, when the Captain cried a salutation to him.

"He was a generous cully while he lived,"
said Jacobus. "And now, 'twixt hawk and
buzzard, he is food for the hoody-crows."

"May I never come to say the same at your
gallows'-foot, Captain," said I.

"Amen!" rejoined Jacobus, piously.

Soon after, turning to the right, we rode
through Wandsworth, westwards to Lambeth,
where the murdered Archbishop's Palace loomed
across the marsh-flats, thence to London Bridge ;
and so, for the first time in my life I set foot in
London Town. I do not know to what I had
looked forward; but the narrow, dim-lighted streets
and the close air struck me with a sense of outrage
and indecency. After winding through a maze
of mean and noisome lanes and alleys, we came out
upon a long thoroughfare, which, so the Captain
informed me, was Fleet Street, where was the Globe
Tavern, and there we drew rein for the night.

VII

THE BELL–MAN OF SAINT SEPULCHRE'S

SO soon as we had supped, the unwearying Jacobus announced that he must pay a visit to a certain lady of his acquaintance, and would have me to accompany him. Accordingly we repaired to a house but two doors off, which was lighted up as if for a festival.

"Captain," I said, "what place is this?"

"The home of a gaudy temptation, boy, the vestibule to ruined fortunes : a magical palace where time is not, for a man may live a lifetime in a moment, and Adam's curse is abrogated, in virtue of a handful of painted cards. Didst never take a fit o' the cards, Anthony? But of course you would not do 't," said the Captain, attempting the ironical.

"'T is a nice business to indulge on the left hand, without punishing on the right, as the proverb goes," I returned.

The Bell-Man of Saint Sepulchre's

"Come," said Jacobus, "try to forget, once again, that y' are no Bible-mad evangelist, and to remember that we are about King's business. I desire you to take particular heed of the conversation : there cannot be too many checks on the bridle of this sort of cattle."

There was no need to knock, for lounging in the doorway was a slatternly down-at-heel wench who greeted Jacobus in terms of familiarity.

"You will find Mrs. Moll at her accompts," she added, and the Captain, who seemed to know the place, walked upstairs to the first-floor, where there were doors in front and upon the left hand. A great noise of talk, laughter, and the clink of glasses came from behind the door in front ; but it was upon the other that Jacobus knocked twice in a particular manner. A voice cried out to us to enter, and upon opening the door we found ourselves in a panelled room of moderate size and good proportion. Lights burned upon the high wooden mantel, and a sole candle stood upon the polished table at the side of the fire, illuminating the face of one who sat smoking a long clay pipe, behind a great brass-bound ledger which lay open next a bottle and a half empty glass. At first I could not determine whether the singular monster who rose as we entered were male or female, Michael or Diabolus : for the sleek countenance was that of a sly, good-humored, evil woman ; while the doublet and slashed gaskins might have served the turn of a needy sloven of a gentleman : but the Captain's greeting informed me.

"Give you good-den, Mrs. Mary. This gentleman, my friend, and I would be glad of a piece of a talk with you upon certain affairs."

"With all my heart, Captain," responded Moll Cutpurse, in a voice harsh yet insinuating, which put me mind of a snail crawling upon a window-pane. "Y' are ever welcome to my poor house. Methought you would to Rumvile,[1] so soon as I heard that poor Mr. Armorer would be shoving the tumbles from the Checquers[2] to Tyburn."

"Is the date appointed ?" asked Jacobus.

"The day after to-morrow, I have sure news. Such a mighty pretty, civil young gentleman, too, and such a way with the wenches

[1] London.
[2] Whipped at the cart's tail from Newgate.

as he hath. Well, well! Holborn Hill is the road to glory for such as we, Captain, be it soon or be it late. But sit ye down, gentlemen, draw to the fire, and what will ye drink now?"

"A cup of Rosa Solis for me," answered the Captain.

I had no mind to drink in neighborly fashion in such a house, but a glance from Jacobus told me it were best for us; and, as civilly as I could, I said I would have the same. Mrs. Cutpurse rose, and crossing the room with her man's stride, she flung aside a heavy curtain which hung on the wall to the right of the door by which we had entered, disclosing a leaded casement brightly painted with a curious, lewd design, which gave upon the room beyond. As the woman opened the window a broken torrent of talk and shrill laughter flowed upon our ears, mingled with the crazy notes of a song. Mrs. Cutpurse leaned over the sill and called for the liquor, and, moving a pace, I looked over her shoulder, seized with an eager curiosity. A company of gallants sat about the lighted tables: many were playing at cards, entirely sunk in a watchful absorption; while others, flushed and disordered, were drinking and noisily singing. One uplifted gentleman, with a foot upon the table and a wine-glass held askew in his shaking hand so that the liquor spilled, was chanting a song of the Rump with a very scandalous bob to it.

"Will you not join my merry company assembled, my pretty gentleman, while I discuss with the sober Captain?" asked Mrs. Moll, turning to me with a leer, and ran on in her horrible voice, that rasped upon me like a finger-nail on silk, in force to cajole me. But I answered very shortly, turning my back broad upon her; and the liquor being brought, she hasped the window, drew the curtain, and without any more words sat down again at the table, facing the Captain; while I drew a chair to the fire on the opposite side of the hearth.

"At your service, Captain," said Mrs. Cutpurse, cheerily, with unruffled composure. "You want a gob of money, as usual, I take it. Well, now, and what is the sum?"

"Mrs. Cutpurse, I should explain to you Mr. Langford, keeps her moneys at the charges of the Commonwealth," said the Captain.

The Bell-Man of Saint Sepulchre's

" 'T is the only privilege, perhaps, she shares with Oliver, as the similarity of their hand of write is the single point of likeness between them. But the last, it is true, Mrs. Cutpurse shares with every one who have skill to write at all."

Indeed, this female iniquity was so accomplished a forgeress that upon several occasions the Commonwealth Treasury honored her drafts for large sums, supposing them to be genuine ; until at length Cromwell was forced to invent a private mark.

Captain Jacobus then proceeded to unfold his proposal : which was, that Mrs. Cutpurse should repair on the morrow to Wallingford House with a forged warrant for a thousand pounds, and that during the night following, the Captain should bring to her ample security for that amount — in what form did not transpire — and exchange it for the money. Mrs. Cutpurse put questions and made conditions with the acerb shrewdness of a scrivener ; and that business was speedily despatched. The Captain then went on to disclose the details of a scheme to be carried through during the

next four-and-twenty hours, in which Mrs.
Cutpurse was to bear a main part. Meanwhile, I sat back in the shadow, taking careful
heed of their talk. The devil's-din in the next
chamber went on, with now and again a ring
of broken glass, a cascade of tipsy laughter, or a
swinging song with a roaring chorus. I found
time between-whiles to marvel at the romantical volutions of circumstance : at this hour I
should have been riding homewards across
Salisbury Downs, my head full of sunbright,
happy memories ; and the field of dark and
rolling hills, domed with the sparkling sky,
rose before me. I recalled the thymy scent of
the night-wind breathing in my face ; and looking round the close chamber, which seemed to
copy the vicious aspect of its owner, a sense of
intolerable sickness took me, and I got suddenly
to my feet.

At the same moment the Captain came to an
end and rose also. We made our way out of
the house by a narrow back stairway which led
us into an alley as dark as pitch. I could discern nothing but a confusion of roofs against a
jagged piece of sky, where the stars were wink-

ing. But the Captain went confidently forward, and two or three sharp turns brought us into Fleet Street, which was dimly lighted at long intervals by oil-lamps slung on chains betwixt the houses. The place was deserted save for a few prowling shadows, and in the distance, the glimmering lanterns of the watch. The clock of Saint Dunstan's was clanging twelve as we reached the door of our tavern ; and upon the last reverberation followed the far-away scream of a woman, a confused shouting, and the clash of steel.

"Alsatians serenading," quoth Jacobus, "down in Whitefriars yonder. You would not hold our friend Mrs. Cutpurse in all points as the fruit of the Holy Seed, perhaps ; but were I to take you to houses I wot of in Alsatia, you would think her bagnio a conventicle, by comparison. But come in to bed, my young friend. I shall to sleep like a dog, till nature wakes me ; and I would counsel you to the same, for it's little enough sleep you'll get presently."

But I lay long awake that night, for I was over-weary. The liquor I had drunk had set my brain clear as a lighted room, wherein I acted over and over again the scenes of the past three days; and when at last I fell on sleep a little before dawn, the scream of the woman rang in my dreams, and I seemed to see her fleeing through narrow mazes, pursued by ruffians; and try as I might, I could never come up to her, nor see her face.

It was high noon before we rose next day; and after a great and choice meal we set forth into the streets. Here I speedily grew discomfortably angry with the jostling tide of wayfarers, who made nothing of elbowing a man into the kennel without so much as a word; while the horrible clamor of the flat-capped 'prentices crying their masters' wares upon the pavement filled my ears; and the warm fetid smell of the place, like that of a swamp, nauseated me to the gizzard. We passed down Fleet Street and up Ludgate Hill to Paul's. At the corner of the Churchyard the Captain showed me, as he had done at Winchester by Brother Jedediah, the low-browed house and close-shuttered shop of Brother Emanuel, and his gilded sign decently draped in black sarcenet.

The Bell-Man of Saint Sepulchre's

Walking in Paul's for awhile, we found it crowded with bargaining merchants, bustling cits, gallants and their lasses, more like a cried fair than a temple of God. Thence we took our way down Blow-Bladder Street to Newgate Prison, a part of which, as it served for the City gate-house, stood on either side of the road. The buildings were tall and narrow, with a great door in the centre, and a single tier of plain barred windows rising on each side. A little beyond is Giltspur Street, which, branching into two on either side of a pile of buildings at its junction with Newgate Street, turns off towards Smithfield. The church of Saint Sepulchre stands at the further corner. These particulars, together with the relative positions of the adjacent streets and side alleys, I must learn by heart, in view of the night's work ; and to this end we paced about and about, backwards and forwards, until I had the tract of huddled houses bounded by the Fleet Prison and Paul's on the west and east respectively, Fleet Street on the south, and Smithfield on the north, clear as a map in my head. By that time it had fallen dusk, and we returned to the Globe Tavern to dine. As we sat at meat Captain Jacobus impressed upon me the order for the night's enterprise with great particularity. The first thing to do was to get speech of the condemned highwayman, Mr. Nicholas Armorer, who (it will be remembered) had been taken by Cromwell's patrol immediately after having slain Mr. Secretary Thurloe's express from the Low Countries. Now the success of the Penruddock plot depended upon the Government's ignorance thereof; if Armorer had destroyed the mails before he was overpowered, all was so far well; but if, on the other hand, they had fallen into the hands of his captors, the whole plan of operations must be altered. The prisoner, and the prisoner alone, could give us this most necessary news; and if the Captain succeeded in winning to him, Jacobus would at the same time convey a parcel of weapons with which he might make good his escape. To this end Jacobus intended to personate the Bell-Man of Saint Sepulchre's, who administered the consolations of religion to all condemned criminals the night before their execution.

For a certain Mrs. Elizabeth Elliott, whose

son, having been condemned to death and at
the last moment reprieved by the King's
clemency, dying some few years since, had in
gratitude bequeathed a sum of money to the
Parish of Saint Sepulchre's, to the intent that
they should find a man forever, who, betwixt the
hours of eleven and twelve the night before the
prisoner's execution, should go under Newgate,
giving warning of his presence by the solemn
ringing of a hand-bell. He was then to put
them in mind of their imminent end by the
reading of certain prayers and pious exhortations.
Now Mrs. Moll Cutpurse had undertaken to
entice the Bell-Man into her house that evening ; the Captain would take from him his
book of devotions, and habit himself in the
great blue cloak with silver buttons in which
the Bell-Man officiated. My part in the plot
was, briefly, to withdraw the crowd from about
the Captain in order to secure him a few
moments of solitude wherein to accomplish his
design. I must then return to the house of
Mrs. Cutpurse and there await Jacobus, who,
it seemed, had another business in hand. When
I learned the details, I owned to myself the

design wore a singularly desperate aspect; but there was no question of thievery this time; and I promised myself, at the least, some pleasurable excitement. Nor was I in any sense disappointed in that expectation.

The dinner eaten, we primed our pistols afresh, and, fully armed, masked, and cloaked, made a circuit and entered the bagnio by the privy door. We found the lady flauntingly apparelled in purple Lucca velvet, much bedecked and bejewelled; and I misliked her more than ever. Dressed as a man she appeared merely monstrous, but clothed as a woman she seemed to insult her sex. She led us straightway into a little apartment that opened off the room in which she had entertained us the night before; and there, all fallen together in a great chair by the fire, a huge, gross man with a tangle of red hair lay in a slumber so profound that, had he been dead, he could have been no more insensible of our approach. A black-jack stood on the floor at his side, empty; and a faint, pungent odor hung in the air.

"He drinks a mighty potation," remarked Mrs. Moll, "and after the way I mixed it, I'll warrant him to slumber through the trumpet-blast of the great Archangel.''

The Captain doffed his hat, and, picking up the Bell-Man's blue camlet cloak from behind the door, put it on and pulled the hood over his head. Searching in the lining, he presently drew forth a thin volume bound in brown leather, and conned it swiftly through.

"There is a cursedly scant measure of the farrago," said he. "You must be mighty quick, Anthony, or I shall have to spin prayers out of my head like an Independent. This is a job would have better suited the Golden Farmer."

Upon leaving the house, we found awaiting us at the door the Bell-Man's open cart, to which a big black mule was harnessed. A 'prentice-lad stood at the brute's head, and a number of idlers had gathered round. I took the reins, the Captain tossed the boy a coin, and climbing into the cart, we set off towards Saint Sepulchre's upon Snow Hill. The mule went at a funeral pace ; and finding that no persuasion prevailed upon it, I desisted therefrom, supposing that the beast was trained to the proper custom.

The crowd increased momentarily, and began to surround us, until by the time we descried the swinging lanterns of the Watch at the corner by the church, the multitude must have numbered some two or three hundred. Many in the procession carried links; so that the red gleam flitted from casement to casement of the houses on either hand, lit strongly and struck into vividness faces here and there among the throng, while a world of shadows danced overhead, amid the smoke and glare. At Saint Sepulchre's, the Watch, with shouldered bills, brown or bright, fell in among the crowd; and in this order we arrived at Newgate.

Stopping the cart in the middle of the road, I jumped down and began to work my way through the throng, which strove to press close. The glare of the torches flickered upon the grisly walls and tiers of black barred windows; looking back, I saw the Captain rise to his feet and open his book.

"Gentlemen, are you awake?" he cried, in a great voice, scanning the grim fronts of the prison to left and right.

I had but time to catch an answering cry

CLIMBING INTO THE CART, WE SET OFF TOWARDS
ST. SEPULCHRE'S.

from within the condemned hold, when I was clear of the press, and running hot-foot back to Giltspur Street. Reaching the back of the square of houses on either side of which Giltspur Street branches into Newgate Street, I paused, and looked about; for it was in this place, well within hearing of Newgate, that I purposed to raise a hue-and-cry. The street was deadly quiet, so that my footsteps made an extraordinary commotion; and so far as I could discern by the faint starlight and the glimmer of a lamp at a little distance, not so much as a cat was stirring. Stepping out into the roadway, which here formed a small open space of triangular shape, I opened my mouth and shouted " Fire, ho ! Fire ! "

The word had an effect, immediate and unexpected. From the shadows a figure detached itself and came swiftly towards me. As it drew nearer, I made out the form of a man something smaller and slighter built than myself; the face under the broad hat was closely muffled.

"Where is the fire, sir ? " inquired the stranger, eagerly, peering about at the dark and silent houses.

This was a difficulty I had not anticipated. "Why, here, sir," I answered. "Do you not see it? Help me to raise the alarm, then. There is no time to be lost;" and I was fetching my breath for another alarum when the stranger clapped a hand upon my mouth.

"Y' are mad, or jesting," he said, angrily. "There is no fire. And I want the street kept quiet."

"And I want it raised," I returned, pinioning him. "Leave me be, my little man, or I will break you in pieces."

My gallant struggled furiously, and dealing him a kick that sent him headlong, I began to halloo at the top of my pipe. In another moment casements were flung open, night-capped heads bobbed out, and voices from all quarters took up the cry. My gentleman picked himself from the kennel and ran upon me with naked blade.

"Look, then!" I cried; and, obeying my outstretched arm, he stopped and turned, then, with an inarticulate cry, dashed forward.

For at that very instant, to my extreme amazement, I spied a light tongue of flame

amid a spiral of smoke upon the thatched roof
of the house opposite to me, then another and
another, and before I could move, the place
was burning like a torch. My task was accomplished, with a vengeance; the crowd came
pouring through the narrow streets on either
side the central block in the midst of which
my house was blazing. I felt as if I had set
light to it myself, and fought my way towards
the flames with intent to do what I might to
extinguish them. Half-way through the crowd
I met my young gallant carrying a wench in
his arms, the people making way for him.

"O you!" he cried, stopping. "I think
you must be a witch or the Devil. I have
been watching the place all night, and how
could it have caught fire? Make way, sir.
You shall not stop me!"

I never saw a boy so mad with excitement,
and as I stepped aside to let him pass I noted
that the girl was fully dressed as if for riding.
Then my imminent appointment with the Captain coming to mind, I freed myself from the
roaring mobile and took my way back to Fleet
Street. As I walked my head cooled, and it

Captain Jacobus

broke upon my understanding that had it not been for the singular chance of the conflagration (an accident, perhaps, of the young lady's vigil), I had come extraordinary near to upsetting a deeply-schemed plan of elopement.

VIII

MR. AND MRS. CUTPURSE

LOATH as I was to enter the gambling den, I feared to loiter in the street; and finding the privy door upon the latch, I mounted the dark stairs to the room we had but lately left. Mrs. Moll was sitting at ease by the fire, pipe in mouth, a glass of schnapps at her elbow, and greeted me with her customary offensive complaisance.

"I am glad, indeed, to see you safe and sound, Mr. Langford. And how have you sped, sir, and what will you drink while you tell me? Canary, Rhenish, Xeres, burnt claret, sack, Rosa Solis — What you will?"

"Nothing, I thank you," I said, for although I was mighty dry, the remembrance of Mrs. Cutpurse's hospitality to the Bell-Man stuck in my throat.

"Well, indeed, y' are a queer cove of a young gentleman as ever I saw in the world. Ye will not drink, nor, I dare swear, would ye dice. Pray, sir, how do you live? Nay, never look black. Take no note of an old woman's quirks, but sit ye down, and tell me, an ye will, how go matters."

In a few words I related the night's adventures so far as I knew them. Mrs. Cutpurse heard me with infinite glee.

"Mr. Armorer will 'scape the gallows yet,'" she cried. "Jacobus is a clever rogue. He maketh an ill enemy; I would never cross him by my will. And why? Because I am honest? No, for I am not honest,—'t is a dull commodity, honesty, and one I could never find any use for. But I am afraid of him, Mr. Langford; and fear is a stout bond for square dealing."

I muttered a civil word in reply; this trifling encouragement was enough for Mrs. Cutpurse, who, being perhaps a little disguised in liquor, began a manner of talk the like of which I had never heard. A kind of poisonous magic dwelt in her tongue; so that as this brazen schoolmistress of sin with the cunning eye held discourse, life and the world as she conceived of them passed before me like scenes in a playhouse : gross, tragical, outrageous, and farcical by turns ; always blindly base, yet intertwisting throughout this monstrous web of passion, avarice, and mis-doing, a thread of natural, human kindliness and shrewd good-humor. I could see that Mrs. Moll was one of your born praters ; set a piece of listening intelligence in front of her, and she asked no more ; the woman was sublimely happy, and would talk until her head was clean empty. The matter of her discourse cannot be put down here ; but it fascinated me, so that I did not hear the latch lift, and only a sense of some one looking at me caused me to turn my head, to catch a glimpse of a man just disappearing out of the door. Swift as he was, I had time to recognize the burly figure and white locks of Mul-Sack.

"What is it?" demanded Mrs. Cutpurse, whose back was towards the door, turning quickly as she spoke.

"'T is nothing," I said. "I but fancied I heard the door open," for the stealthy demeanor of the King of the Beggars aroused my suspicions. 119

"I heard nothing," Mary said. "What could it have been?" and rising, she went to the door, opened it, put her head into the passage, then closed it again, returned to the hearth, and stood looking keenly down at me.

"There is no one there," said she. "Perhaps your fancy plays you tricks at times, Mr. Langford?"

"Why often," I replied, sleepily, and yawned. At this moment a distant rumble of wheels broke upon our ears, grew rapidly louder, and was presently mingled with a clatter of galloping hoofs. "The Captain at last," cried Mrs. Cutpurse, and ran down the stairs, where I could hear her unbarring the door. The sounds ceased abruptly, a hasty foot pounded on the stair, and the Captain, red with hurry, burst into the room, a bulky sack upon his shoulder.

"The Bell-Man," he cried, dumping his burden on the table. "Quick, man, out with him, neck and heels. The Watch are upon us hot-foot."

Snatching a candle, I flung open the door of the inner room, while the Captain tore off the blue camlet cloak. The Bell-Man was still slugging in a dog-sleep, just as we had left him. I took his shoulders, Jacobus took his heels, and we bundled him down stairs, hove him into the cart, and flung his cloak upon him in a breathless hurry. Mrs. Moll, who had been standing at the mule's head, whipped into the house, and as the Captain dealt the beast a sounding kick which started it at a gallop, I heard the door slam and the clank of iron bars falling into their sockets.

We turned to find ourselves locked out. At the bottom of the street a clump of lanterns and glinting weapons was advancing at a round pace. There was small time for consideration; in three minutes, or less, a dozen of the Watch armed with six-foot bills would be upon us.

"Bilked, are we!" cried Jacobus, with an oath. "Round to the back!"

"Did you know that Mul-Sack was in the house," I asked him, as we ran.

"Who?" exclaimed the Captain.

"Mul-Sack. I saw him."

We gained the dark archway leading to the network of alleys that gave upon the back door of the bagnio. Peering out, we had the pleasure of beholding the whole body of Watchmen till past the end of the street, and heard them clamping into the distance.

"That's serious," said Jacobus. "I can check and bridle the man, or his villanous wife. But the two together — no, I don't like it, Anthony."

"His wife?"

"Ay, Mr. and Mrs. Cutpurse, or Mr. and Mrs. Mul-Sack, which you will, and plenty of choice beside. But now to try the other door. There's a thousand pounds' worth of spoils in their clutches, and I doubt me of treasons and stratagems."

Upon trying the latch, we found it fast. A casement clinked open above our heads, and, looking up, the Captain had but just time to clutch my arm and step swiftly aside, before a bucketful of scalding water descended upon the spot where we had been standing. With an oath, Jacobus drew a pistol and snapped it; and although the spark fell upon damp powder, the window shut sharply.

"We will get in, by God," whispered Jacobus, as he reprimed his weapons. "Fire at the lock with both your pistols, then charge the door."

I looked hastily to my priming, then, standing close against the door, presented my weapons. Jacobus did the same with one of his, holding the other in reserve. He gave the word; there was a flash and shattering explosion; the door went down before our united weight, and we were inside. At the same moment a dark figure appeared upon the stairhead above. Jacobus fired on the instant, and the man tumbled forward with a scream, his pistol exploding in his hand. As we dashed up the stair, the door of Mrs. Cutpurse's room shut to, and we heard the bolts click.

"Down with it," cried Jacobus.

I ran at the door, which burst inwards, tripping over the fallen man in my hurry, so that I tumbled headlong into the room amid a ruin of woodwork. Jacobus trampled right over me, and I picked myself up to find him strenuously engaged with Mrs. Moll, who was wielding a long rapier with the utmost fury and a great deal of dexterity.

"Disarm her with a cloak," cried Jacobus.

Flinging my mantle across the blades, I pinioned the lady from behind ; and it was all I could do to restrain her passionate struggles without maiming her. But Jacobus slipped off his belt, and we tied her wrists with a garter, and buckled her into a chair, where she began to vociferate curses with diabolical fluency. Victory was ours, but there was scant leisure for contemplation. The other inmates of the house would raise a hue-and-cry in another moment ; already we heard a bustle and the noise of opening doors above stairs. The Captain caught up his sack from the table and ran out of the house ; and, seeing a stout leathern valise beside it, upon a sudden impulse I tucked it under my arm and followed. Mul-Sack lay where he had fallen, and the stairs were slippery with his blood.

"The black, arrant, filthy scoundrels !" said the Captain, as we twisted and turned through by-ways. "They would 'a robbed his Majesty of my hardly-earned gains without so much as a God-a-mercy. What have you there, boy ?"

"I don't know — 't is cursedly heavy."

"Well, we must lug our burdens yet awhile. God send we meet not the rascals of the Watch."

Mr. and Mrs. Cutpurse

So soon as the Captain judged us out of danger of pursuit, we slackened pace to a brisk walk, setting our course to arrive at the back premises of the Globe Tavern. I told Jacobus of my adventure.

"Well, I would not tell that story too often," said he. "You might not always receive credence. Truth is a fantastical divinity. But y' are an admirable scarefire ! The street cleared in a twinkling, just as I reached the benediction. I could see Nick's face plain behind the bars of a window ten or twelve feet up, cheek by jowl with a scab of jailer."

" ' In case the prisoner hath any doubts on his sinful soul, of which I may resolve him,' I cried, ' I will come within convenient earshot ; ' and with that drove the pulpit right under the cill.

"Quick as lightning Nick stretched his hands through the bars, manacled as they were, as low as he could reach, and standing on tip-toe I gave him a naked girdle-knife. Listening, I heard certain graveyard sounds within ; and forth looks Nick again.

" ' I 've killed him,' says he.

" 'Where are the Flanders despatches?' I asked.

" 'Gone to the four winds,' he answered.

"Whereupon I gave him pistols and a file and sundry articles, and left him with my blessing to work his way out of the Checquers as best he might, and drove softly away to Paul's Churchyard. I spare your feelings, my young friend, I will not tell you what I did under the shadow of Paul's. The business ('t was King's business) I carried thorough-stitch without a let, until the Watch came loitering round the corner of Paternoster Row just as the Bell-Man was filling his pulpit. There would have been no cause to alarm had not that devil of a mule refused to budge. For all I could do he stood immovable as a statue, till I drew sword and goaded him like an ox; and then he shot off like a culverin, and near tore the heart out of me with pulling. I thought we should have gone to hell without a stop; but the fiend halted himself of his own accord at Mrs. Moll's. I suppose the drouthy Bell-Man had taught him the habit. And, after all, lifelekins! we were woundy near losing the whole pack. I would I had known King Mul-

Mr. and Mrs. Cutpurse

Sack was on the night sneak. Well, set the scars against the booty and cry quits," concluded Jacobus.

"And is he, then, Mrs. Moll's husband?" I asked.

"Ay," returned the Captain. "They were married over the broom. I was at the wedding, and gave the bride away, while the Patrico joined their hands across a headless fowl, and the groomsman poured a gage of nun-booze over the bridegroom's head. And this evening the pair would have robbed and murdered me! Save a thief from the gallows and he'll cut your throat, Anthony," quoted Jacobus, irrelevantly.

By this time we had reached the gates of the Globe stable-yard; as we had settled the score over-night, we had nothing to do but to rouse the ostler and get our nags saddled. In a few moments we found ourselves once more horsed and on the road, with the plunder gained by the night's adventures securely strapped upon the crupper. We were to proceed straightway, said the Captain, to the Earl of Rochester, who had his lodging very private near Whitehall. As we paced slowly and cautiously along back streets, I turned to reflection upon the events of that turbulent night; the remembrance of old Mul-Sack prone upon his face stuck mightily in my head; and like a sword-prick out of the dark, it flashed upon me that yet a third time I had been art and part in an outrageous robbery. And again, I could not for the life of me see how I could have done other than I did. There seemed a perverse fate in it; and I resolved to clear my mind of incipient repentance, and transferred, in my accompt with Heaven, the sin to the close-written debit of Cromwell.

Moreover, I had come to sojourn in places, and to taste of experiences, extremely foreign to the principles of my father's son. I had made acquaintance with the reverse of the coin, — the other side of the image God has stamped upon the mixed metal of humanity, — and observed, with some surprise, and some reservations, the stirring within me of new and catholic sympathies.

IX

I BECOME KING'S MESSENGER

IT must have been near three of the clock in the morning when we drew rein at the door of a mansion that stood midway down a narrow street giving upon the river, as I could discern by the tremulous reflections of the stars upon a moving gray bank between the black cliffs of building. Dismounting, we secured our horses to the wrought iron-work that supported the extinguisher-cap for links. The Captain knocked upon the panel, at first softly, then with more insistence. A window opened overhead, and stepping back, we perceived the head and shoulders of a man in a night-cap, covering us with a petronel.

"Who be you?" he demanded, with a broad south-country accent, "disturbing decent folk in their beds."

9   129

"Let me in, George Penderel," said the Captain.

"There be no one of that name here," returned the other, hastily. "Who be you, I arx again before I fires."

"You have met with a Mr. William Jones, I believe, George," said the Captain. "Well, I bear a message for him. Open, in the name of Mr. William Jones!"

I learned afterwards that this George Penderel was a Royalist trooper, one of those who were art and part at the King's escape after Worcester fight, his Majesty travelling at that juncture under the name of William Jones. The Captain's conjuration was singularly effectual. Mr. Penderel retired instantly from the window; and within a minute we heard him unbarring the door. It was presently opened, and a little, broad man with a big nose, a military cloak wrapped about his naked body, appeared on the threshold, holding a rushlight above his head.

"Give ye good-den, Captain," said he, saluting.

"I have to speak with his lordship, George,"

said Jacobus. "You had best announce me, while we bring in the horses."

Saluting once more, the trooper turned to obey, leaving the rushlight on the floor. By the time we had brought the horses into the square stone hall, where the noise of their tramplings was enough to rouse the parish, Penderel returned, saying that the Earl would see us on the instant, and, carrying our booty with us, we followed the retainer up a broad staircase to a huge shadowy apartment hung with dark tapestry, which seemed to suck up the light of the many candles. The embers of a wood-fire flickered in the chimney by the side whereof stood a great bed with gold-embroidered hangings, and wherein lay my Lord of Rochester, his jolly, red face aglow among the white napery.

"What, Jacobus, my night-hawk, and with a King's ransom on 's back, as I live by bread ! Naught less shall indemnify for the breakage of my beauty-sleep, I promise ye," said the Earl, in a lazy, drawling fashion of his own.

"Y' are too curious of yourself, my Lord Wilmot," returned the Captain, depositing his burden on the table before the fire, and signing me to do the same. "But let that pass, and suffer me to present to you my very worthy copesmate, Mr. Anthony Langford, of Langford."

The Earl shook me heartily by the hand, with a courteous rejoinder; "Y' are heartily welcome, gentlemen," quoth he. "'T is a poor place to receive you in, I fear, but the best a landless lord and a man proscribed may offer at this time. Draw to the fire — prithee, Jack, put on another log — there is liquor on the table. Fill your glass, Mr. Langford — I thank you, yes, if you will be so good. The King, Mr. Langford," and the Earl and I clinked glasses.

"And now to business, my lord," began Jacobus.

"Ay," returned Rochester, "certainly. But I must tell you, Captain — walking adown Giltspur Street yesternoon, I met as pretty a nymph as ever I saw in the world. She hath meeting eyebrows and a sloe-black eye — you know the kind of quean, Jack. I shall walk there to-morrow, and the day after, and every day until I meet with her again. Come with me in the morning, my bold freebooter."

"Y' are but a mad lord," answered the Captain. "Do you take me for Cheffinch?[1] A pox on ye! Here is a kingdom set upon the hazard, and you think of naught but springing a hen o' the game. Come! I have not been hunting and waiting like a dog for many weeks, to be toying with your wanton humors. I tell you, every minute I sit here as good as turns a new thread upon my halter."

"That is because y' are so partial to blood and wounds, Jack," drawled Rochester, with unruffled composure. "Stand and deliver, is your notion of entertainment; mine is another-guess theory. Body o' me! a man must do something to disperse the vapors in this hag-rid city, he would die of sheer psalmody else. Why, the place reeks of Nonconformity; it drones like a vast conventicle. Well, to business then, curse ye. What news from the West?"

Whereupon the Captain put him briefly into possession of affairs, telling him, however,

[1] A creature of the King's.

no more of our adventures than he was necessitated. Meanwhile, I had leisure to observe his lordship, who was a full-faced, handsome man, with the look of a born amorist. He it was (so I have heard), who during his flight with the King after Worcester, would never put on any habit of disguise, saying, " he should look so frightfully in it."

" And what hast got in the bag there?" inquired the Earl, when the tale was ended. " Ye may rest easy," he added, as the Captain rose, and going to the door, shot the bolt ; " the house is empty, save for George the faithful." So Jacobus unloosed the sack, and displayed upon the table a treasure of gold and silver plate, and jewelled gew-gaws, enough to ransom a city.

" 'Sblood !" quoth the Earl, sitting up in bed. " And where did that pretty treasure come from ? "

The Captain maintained a discreet silence ; and, having turned the sack bottom up, he began to unstrap my valise. I looked on with a keen curiosity, but saying nothing. Throwing back the lid, Jacobus took out, one by one, ten full-stuffed leather bags, and set them heavily down a-row. The figures £100 were branded upon each, and, untying one, he took out a handful of his yellow namesakes. "A thousand pound in coin of the realm," said he. So we had not only ransacked Brother Emanuel's shop in Paul's, but plundered the coffers of the Commonwealth and stripped Mrs. Moll of her profits at a blow.

"Odso! and where from, once more?" asked the delighted Rochester.

"Well, my lord, the history, in brief, is as follows," answered Jacobus, sitting down and filling his glass. "I happened to have a small matter of family plate to sell — the gear, in fact, you see before you. 'T is the old story; what cavalier but has flung his plate-chest, spoons, and tankards into the deeps of Neptune after the rest of his goods for the love of his Gracious Majesty? But no more of that. Therefore, I say, I sought out a gripe of my acquaintance and bade him give me the price in gold. This he agreed to do, but as it came about the villain sought to play booty — and failed. Whereupon I took a hand — and succeeded."

Jacobus lay back in his chair, pressing the tips of his stretched fingers lightly together, and gravely regarded the Earl. Their eyes met. Both men smiled.

"I make you my compliments, Jack," said Rochester. "Y' are as arrant a thief and as bold a liar as any in the three kingdoms. 'Oons, but we will dine to-morrow, Jack. I know an ordinary —"

"So do I, my lord," interrupted the Captain; "and the night the King dines in White-hall you and I will drink drunk hand to fist, an his Majesty invite us not, and unless my head be garnishing Temple Bar."

"Y' are perfectly right, Jack," answered Rochester, no jot abashed. "Shall I give you full acquittal for value received on behalf of my Lord Treasurer, who is at this time taking the air of the Low Countries for the good of his health?"

"So, please you, before we part," returned Jacobus, gravely. "And, now, who is to carry mails to the King, my lord? The matter is urgent."

"Whomsoever you please, Captain," replied the easy Earl.

I become King's Messenger

" Mr. Langford, will you?" said Jacobus. So it was settled ; and I doubt not that the Captain had this errand in his eye for me from the first.

" The *Silver Spray* sails from New Key to Flushing with the morning tide," said Rochester. " The master, Captain Powel Revel, who is a trusty rascal, was with me yesterday."

"That will do excellent well," said the Captain. Thereupon the Earl, bidding us to excuse him, rose and dressed himself, and sat down with Jacobus to write despatches to the King. By the time they had finished, the sun was shooting golden shafts through the crevices of the shutters, and we descended to a room beneath, where was spread an ample collation flanked with toasts and tankards, of which the Earl partook full as heartily as we. Then I was given a hundred broad pieces for my peculiar expenses, and entrusted with two hundred for the King, and the mail, which was enclosed in silk and sealed. My instructions were, upon landing at Flushing to repair at once to the sign of the City of Rouen, where I should find Sir John Mennes and Mr. John Nicholas, who would introduce me to his Majesty ; when I was to answer any questions the King might be pleased to ask me, to receive his instructions, particularly as to the date of the Penruddock rising, and to return without delay to the port of Lyme Regis in Dorsetshire, where I should meet Captain Jacobus at a place appointed. Taking leave of the buxom Earl, upon whose shoulders, methought, the cares of state sat extraordinary lightly, I set out on foot, carrying Mrs. Cutpurse's valise and accompanied by the Captain.

The streets sparkled in the sunshine, and a brisk wind ruffled the awnings over the shops, where the noisy 'prentices were busied setting forth their wares. After purchasing a few clothes and necessaries — for I had ridden all this time with no more than I stood in — we proceeded by devious ways to the New Key hard by London Bridge. The river bubbled and swirled under the arches, reaching away like a magical arm into enticing distance between clumps of shipping whose tall masts and webs of rigging rose above the houses. Wherries manned by watermen in gay colored jerkins plied swiftly to and fro across the shining stream, and my heart rose blithely to the adventure. The *Silver Spray*, a bluff-bowed, two-masted craft, was moored against the wharf; the most of her crew were climbing and clinging aloft, engaged upon some business which appeared to me extremely perilous, to which they were directed by a small, stout man with a fringe of black whisker encircling a face like a walnut, who stood shouting on deck. We went aboard at once, and Jacobus, going up to the officer, whispered a word or two in his ear, whereupon he led us down into a tiny cabin. Jacobus made me known to Captain Powel Revel, and a bargain for shipping me as passenger to Flushing was speedily struck. Captain Revel was in his Majesty's pay, and although his ship passed for a merchant bottom he did little but carry the King's servants to and from the Low Countries, — a traffic which the Parliament winked at, Thurloe trusting wholly to his secret service for discovery of treason. The business over, Captain Revel warned Jacobus that he must set sail forthwith to save the tide, and we all three went upon deck.

"Give you good-den, Anthony," said Captain Jacobus, grasping my hand. "We meet again at Lyme." He turned away, leaped ashore, and with a wave of his hand vanished into the press. The moorings were cast off, the ship swung into the current and began to travel, the water rippling under her fore-foot. I leaned upon the bulwarks, looking after Jacobus, oppressed with a sudden sense of loss. Labor and peril shared forge stronger ties than those of kindred, and although I had known the Captain for less than a week I was parting from a friend, — a friend, moreover, whose life was forfeit on a hundred counts, for whom a very trifling misadventure meant the rope and the triple tree, so that the chance of seeing him once more appeared pitifully slender.

But my dolorous meditations were speedily interrupted. Scarce was the ship fairly under way ere there arose a shouting and a bustling on the wharf, and a skiff manned by a couple of water-men, and carrying two passengers, a man and a woman, put off after us in a mighty hurry. Captain Revel thereupon lay to, and the skiff drawing rapidly alongside, the strangers were haled aboard. Both were masked and muffled in cloaks. The man, stepping forward, caught the wrathful Captain by the arm and spoke privily to him. It was none of my business, and I walked forward to be out of earshot; and presently the three disappeared below. When the Captain returned alone upon deck, he vouchsafed me no explanation, nor, although I was curious in the matter, did I question him, reflecting that I was certain to meet the unknown at the next repast. But when dinnertime came the Captain, his mate, and myself were the only persons assembled in the poop cabin. Scarce a word was uttered during the collation — indeed, Captain Revel was one of the silentest men I have ever known. He manifested a positive distaste for conversation. There was a tincture of barbarism, too, in the tarpaulin way of living and being. More than once I observed the Captain to clean his knife upon the hair of his mate, who sat beside him, — an outrage of which the man took no sort of notice, while it put me in a fever lest the Captain, in a moment of forgetfulness, should raise his whittle upon his passenger. I was glad to find myself once more upon deck, where I took great delight in the quiet, bird-like motion of the ship, and the continual alluring change of the landscape on either strand. A shipman's life was a brave business indeed, methought. Soon the sun and the wind and the talking water wrought a drowsiness upon me. I bethought me that I had a night's rest to make up, and, settling myself against a coil of rope, fell speedily dead asleep.

Before I awoke I was aware of a horrible queasy sensation in my inner parts, and opened my eyes upon a darkening steel-blue sky, pricked here and there with a star. The ship was heaving and rolling under me, and a cold wind searched my very marrow. Sitting up with a deadly shudder, my eyes encountered the fierce gaze of a little gentleman reclining miserably against the bulwarks a few feet from me. His face, in spite of its green pallor, I seemed to recollect, as in a dream; and when he spoke it came back to me.

"Ay, Master Scarefire, would you follow me?" he said, in weak angry accents. "So soon as we land, I challenge you to fight me, sir."

I would have laughed, but I was far past mirth; for here was my eloping gallant from Giltspur Street again.

"Put an end to me now," I said. "Run me through and I will thank you."

My gentleman groaned and swore. "I cannot lift a hand," he said, and turned over on his face.

Thereafter followed a night of horror; and it was not until noon next day that we began to get the better of our disorder. By that time we had come in sight of land; a long ridge of yellow sand-bank, beyond a plain of dancing sea, shot with flying colors, and dashed with foam, against a sky of pearl. We had both eaten something, and drank a toss of aqua vitæ, and had come again upon deck. It seemed a senseless thing to quarrel; and at the risk of a serious tumble I crossed to where my angry gallant leaned sulking over the weather taffrail, and laid a hand upon his shoulder.

"Come," I said. "I am sorry I struck you t' other night. Are you for Cæsar? I can see that you are. Well, I was employed on King's business, although I own it did not look like it. Will you shake hands?"

The boy looked at me a moment, then held out his hand.

"Sir," said he, "I accept your apology. We will say no more."

"And how is the young lady?" I inquired. "I trust she is not greatly indisposed."

"But she is, she is," he said very ruefully. "I do not know what I shall do with her."

I consoled the disconsolate lover so well as I might. "And when are you to be married?" I asked, hoping to distract his thoughts from anxiety.

"'T is scarce your business, is it? But doubtless you mean kindly," said the boy, with his chin in his hands. "Perhaps we shall not marry. Think of the risk."

"You should have thought on it before," I said, coldly.

He looked at me sidelong. "After all, you know," he said lazily, "what is the ceremony? A form of words, and a guinea for the parson. I have often thought its quality over-rated."

I was shocked at such sentiments from the mouth of a pretty, smooth-faced boy, and took occasion to read him a homily upon the subject.

I become King's Messenger

I talked for a good while, having nothing else to do, but before I had said all that was in my mind, my companion glanced round, and I saw a new expression flit into his face.

"It may relieve your benevolent but pragmatical conscience, dear sir, to know that we were fast married in Saint Sepulchre's Church yestermorn," said he. "Let me present you to my wife."

I swallowed my discomfiture, and turned to behold — "the wench with the meeting eyebrows and the sloe-black eyes!" The Earl's words ran through my head as a mighty pretty figure of a maiden came balancing delicately towards us. She greeted me very kindly, and we grew mighty friendly. They told me much of their story: how that the bridegroom, Mr. Richard Humphreyville by name, was a Cavalier gentleman and a Roman Catholic, to whom the bride's Puritan parents had refused consent of marriage; and how they determined to cheat the Devil, and to seek their fortune at the Court in exile at Cologne, whither they were immediately bound. In return — with the unthinking confidence of youth — I related something of

my own misfortunes, my quarrel with Manning, and the subsequent confiscation of my
estates. My introduction to the pair had been
something of the strangest; but when we drew
into Flushing Harbor, we parted on the kindliest terms imaginable. Should he discover an
opportunity of advancing my fortunes at the
Court, said the gentleman who the day before
had sought my blood, he would do all a man
might to serve me. Darkly he hinted at the
great personages with whom he had influential
relations; and with the most cordial salutations
this pleasing and singular couple went their
ways, and I saw them no more.

X

A KING IN EXILE

BEFORE quitting the harbor, I turned to see "the last of my sea-sorrow," to filch a pretty phrase of Mr. Shakespeare's. The *Silver Spray* lay moored against the weed-encrusted timbers of the rude landing-stage, her red sails furled, her ropes and spars graven upon the bright sky. But she was shorn of glamour in my regard; the mystery of deep-sea voyaging had resolved itself (for the time) into experience so shocking that I shuddered to recall it, and I bade farewell to the *Silver Spray* as to a sentient being whose acquaintance was more disastrous than desirable.

It was about five in the evening when I left the quays to discover the tavern of the sign of the City of Rouen. The low sun shone full in my eyes, so that I discerned the ornamented, step-gabled buildings, and the strange figures and taking costumes of the Dutch people through a kind of magical splendor; the new, foreign taste of the air struck mighty agreeably upon my senses, and I walked along in a pleasant dream. The Earl of Rochester had directed me precisely to the inn, and I presently came upon it in a square market-place, planted with trees and gay with the awnings of the hucksters' booths. The City of Rouen was a tall building of carven stone, with a projecting porch upheld by caryatid demons, very fantastically wrought; over the portal was a stone cartouch bearing the cognizance cut in basso-rilievo, the towers and ramparts of an ancient Gothic city as if beheld from above, the lines all awry according to the manner of old pictures. Two or three rosy, buxom nymphs, very bravely apparelled in black velvet bodices embroidered with gold and silver, gay flowered shirts, and winged white caps set with bright coins, were chattering and laughing about the entrance. One stepped forward with a courtesy, and addressed me in the Dutch language, to which I replied in English, desiring to be taken to Sir John Mennes and Mr. Nicholas. My damsel caught at the names, and led me up a wide stone stair to an upper room, where I found the gentlemen at dinner. They rose to greet me as I entered; and when salutations had passed, invited me to join them.

Sir John was a trim-built, blue-eyed man of thirty-five or so, with a yellow mustache and hair thinning somewhat on the top; Mr. Nicholas, son to the King's secretary, was a tall, grave, clean-shaven young man of an austere demeanor.

"We are mightily glad to see you, Mr. Langford," said Sir John. "And you bring us good news, I doubt not."

"So far as it goes," I answered, "for the pinch is yet to come;" and I told them the posture of affairs.

"Why the devil," broke out Sir John, "is Oliver not pistolled long since? For the life o' me, I cannot understand it. Here is a scurvy militia-captain grinding the whole country under his heel, all the people hating him like witchcraft,— Royalists, Anabaptists, Fifth Monarchy men, Republicans, and Catholics, all his sworn enemies,— yet not a man of them can come at him!"

"His time is not yet come, as he might say himself," quoth Nicholas.

"Another thing," cried Sir John, with a scowling vehemence, his head upon one side, which I found to be his habit, "why is the King so backward in the plots for his own restoration? You would say he did not care, almost. There's not a man about the Court that is n't neck-deep and fever-hot in caballings and red conspiracies — except the King! Then one party out-plots another party, and so they come to blows, and, six days out of seven, the whole place is by the ears. Of course, it must be so, unless his Majesty takes hold. And why does he not? This business of Penruddock's is the first he has stirred in; and that only as an excuse to get away from Cologne for awhile, I do verily believe," concluded Sir John, with a salvo of oaths.

"'T is a better politician than us all, never doubt that, Sir John," said Nicholas.

"Well, it seems mighty odd to me," returned the other.

Whereupon, over the wine, we plunged into a lengthy argument, which, like all such disputations, led nowhither, and left us a trifle heated and self-important. As for me, when I went to bed that night, rejoicing in down pillows and fine lavender-scented linen, I was in some conceit with myself. I felt that I was playing no small part in the world, moving amid great destinies. I was a person to be reckoned with, a man of momentous experience, strangely removed from the unsophisticated boy who used to ride to and fro from Langford to Salisbury a long time ago. Then the remembrance, never lulled for long, of one sitting desolate in that city awoke within me, and my savory imaginings turned bitter as ashes in my mouth.

By sunrise the next morning I was riding out of Flushing, my valise strapped upon the crupper. Sir John Mennes rode with me. Mr. Nicholas, who stayed at the City of Rouen to be at hand in case further tidings should arrive, lent me his horse. Our way lay along the dikes, the sea upon the one hand and on the other the fair, pied plain stretching away as flat as a table to a wind-bent fringe of poplars. Under the vast gray hollow of the sky the

colors of the fishing-boats on the gray sea, and
the hues of the spring landscape, bore a fresh-
ness like wet paint, very alluring to the eye,
and such as I have never seen in England.
About half-way to Middelburgh we stopped to
drink a tankard of excellent ale at a little, pretty
inn, standing solitary and half-hidden among the
sand-dunes, with a bloom like a peach upon its
ancient stonework and steep-tiled roofs.   As we
rode to the door I glanced up by chance and
caught a glimpse of a face peering from an upper
window.   It was gone in a twinkling, and before I could distinguish the features.   I thought
little of it at the time, but the afterclap brought
the circumstance to mind.

Within an hour after quitting the wayside
inn we were riding along the humming quays of
Middelburgh. A carillon from the Abbey tower
that over-lapped the roofs rose and fell in a
silver fountain of cadences ; great bluff galleons
were lading and unlading with all manner of
merchandise ; the street was thronged with the
alert cheery Hogan-Mogans ; and methought I
had never beheld a town so clean, thriving, and
sumptuous.   Stopping presently at a tall house

of rich appearance Sir John dismounted and, giving me his bridle, knocked upon the door. He was admitted by a serving-man bearing the Ormond badge, and I was left to endure some of the longest minutes of my existence. For I, Anthony Langford, was about to hold audience face to face with the King his Majesty : the thought seemed to dissolve my inwards ; my vision blurred, and I could hear my heart beating.

When Sir John at last returned with the lackey, who took the horses, he must have apprehended my distress.

" What, man ! " he cried. " Take heart of grace. His Majesty is a very pleasant gentleman ; he waits for you now. . . . Y' are forgetting your mails, are you not ? "

In truth, I think I had forgotten my own name ; but so soon as we had fairly entered the room where was the King, my composure returned to me in some measure. I saw a stately gentleman with great dark eyes under black arching brows, and a wide, full-lipped mouth ; his expression was at once melancholy and whimsical. Sir John Mennes presented me to

153

his Majesty, who greeted me with a smiling manner of easy courtesy, giving me his hand to kiss.

"I do remember your father, Mr. Langford," said the King. "He unhappily lost his life in the King, my father's, service — in the affair at Alresford, was it not? And his son, it seems, is bent upon treading that same perilous path of loyalty!"

"'T is the road to honor, sire," I answered.

"And to red herrings in exile, by your leave, Mr. Langford; to present pinching and a future dark and problematical," returned the King, cheerfully. "Well, sir, to the business in hand. Is all in readiness for the date appointed?"

"The date? What date, sire?" I stammered, taken aback.

"The eighteenth of April, man. Did not my express reach my Lord of Rochester?" asked his Majesty, with some impatience.

The words struck upon my hearing like a knell; my wedding-day had been fixed for that day; and murmuring in my confusion that I had not heard — doubtless 't was all contained in the

mails I had the honor to bring — unstrapped my
valise, set the bags of gold upon the table, and,
kneeling, presented the Earl of Rochester's
despatch. The King broke the seal and hastily
perused the letter.

"Ah, the bowls run their old bias, I do
perceive! Contrary winds — messenger de-
layed — plans disordered," said his Majesty,
looking up and addressing Sir John Mennes and
another gentleman (the Marquis of Ormond, as
I discovered afterwards), who seemed to be in
attendance upon the King.

The Marquis swore blasphemously, and
began a question; but the King held up his
slender, jewelled hand, and continued reading.
His Majesty was leaning against the stone
mullion of the great window, the casement of
which stood open; beyond his dark profile rose
a far prospect of sea, melting into pearly mist
and studded with slanting red sails; and a fancy
came across me, that Charles II., loitering
thus upon the shore of the dividing main, stood
but at a pause in his destinies; and that some
day, be it soon or be it late, he should embark
upon a flowing tide, and carry sail till the cord-

age cracked in a fair wind that should bear him to a golden restoration.

"And so you have been riding with Captain Jacobus, Mr. Langford," said the King, when he had finished the mail. "You shall tell me of your adventures over a bottle before we part. Odso! The King's gentlemen spend merrier days than his long-suffering Majesty. If I were to take the road and wreak a little private vengeance on the Roundheads, there would be a pretty hue-and-cry, and God's vicegerent would be cut off incontinent in his prime of manhood! . . . Do you know aught of a certain Mr. John Manning, Mr. Langford?" asked his Majesty, suddenly, to my surprise.

"I know him well, sire," I answered.

"And where is he now?" asked the King, looking at me.

I replied that I knew naught of his movements, save that he had left Salisbury some weeks since.

"Why did he leave?" asked the King.

I hesitated. "Well, the truth of it is, we had a little disagreement, sire," I said.

"About what?" persisted his Majesty, curiously. 156

A King in Exile

"A piece of a lawsuit," said I.

"A piece of a — ?" repeated the King, with an indescribable accent. "Why, very well, Mr. Langford," he went on. "You must forgive me this particularity; for the truth of it is this Manning has much to do with the business in hand. You would say he is a loyal gentleman?"

"I know of naught to the contrary, sire," I answered; and no more did I; nor had I right to formulate my vague suspicions.

"The matter, then, stands thus," the King went on. "You must be well aware, Mr. Langford, that our exchequer, in these unhappy times, is totally empty. In fact, sir, there is no exchequer; and the privy purse would be in an ill way had you not been so good, I see, as to act convoy to supplies. Now, my Lord Wilmot tells me that our incomparable Jacobus has placed in his hands a large sum (I cannot at all imagine how he came by it; you shall enlighten me presently, Mr. Langford); yet there are the troops of the north as well as those of the south to pay, and this cannot suffice. Whereupon Mr. Manning obligingly comes to

157

our assistance — with this magical prescription," and the King took a folded paper from his breast and handed it to me. Upon the inside of the paper were three impressions of an antique head in white wax. "Each of these seals, saith Manning, represents one thousand broad pieces," pursued his Majesty, "which will immediately be given to any person presenting the token at a certain house in Salisbury, upon the condition that the city is first in the hands of the Royalists. The house in question — correct me if I am wrong, Marquis — the house in question stands three doors from the Poultry Cross in the market-place, upon the left hand looking north. Why, man, what has taken thee?" demanded my royal instructor, breaking off.

For I stood bewildered; the King had described the place of Mayor Phelps's abode. It was indeed possible that Mr. Phelps, wealthy, Royalist at heart, and cognizant of the projected rising, had, in my absence, planned such a scheme with Manning; yet I could not think it likely; and it flashed across me, adding to my confusion, that the sum named coincided with the amount of Barbara's dowry. But, again, supposing that Manning were playing for his own hand, it outwent my wit to imagine how such method could serve his end; and yet the affair smelled of treason.

I looked up helplessly. The King was whistling a dance tune through his teeth, with his eyes upon my face.

"If you have aught in your mind, Mr. Langford," said he, gravely, " prithee speak it out. 'T is a matter that concerns the State;" and I straightway resolved to tell the whole truth.

"I crave your pardon, sire. I know the house, which is that of Mr. Phelps, Mayor of the city, a stanch man and well affected to your Majesty. I would put my hand in the fire for Richard Phelps, yet I own I have a doubt upon the matter, for the last time I saw Mr. Manning, when we were both upon a visit to the house, he parted from Mr. Phelps in anger; and soon afterwards he quitted Salisbury, nor have I seen him since — although, of course, he might have returned since my own departure from the city."

"And the quarrel with this worthy Mr. Phelps of whom you speak — was that upon a piece of a — ay, a piece of a lawsuit, also?" asked his Majesty, gently.

I felt my ears grow hot; but there was no help for it; I had to clear the hedge.

"The plain truth of it is, sire, Mr. Manning and myself were both suitors for the hand of Mr. Phelps's daughter; and she preferred — for all I know — the worser man. Mr. Manning, as was very natural, felt himself a little slighted; there were some hasty words passed, and that is the whole of the matter."

His Majesty chuckled, and the two gentlemen laughed outright.

"I thought we should arrive at the lady before we had done," observed the King. "I begin to have a glimmering of the case. Mr. Langford, prithee proceed."

"There is no more to say, your Majesty, save that soon after the Parliament confiscated my estates and would have laid me by the heels, had not Captain Jacobus warned me. Then I took the road with the Captain, listed myself as volunteer under Colonel Penruddock, and —

and so here I am, your Majesty," I concluded lamely.

"Ay, ay," said the King, kindly. "Well, better days will come, man. As to this Manning — where is Mr. Manning at this time, Sir John ?"

"Two days agone he came spurring to the City of Rouen," replied Sir John Mennes. "He would have pulled the house about our ears, because we would not tell him where to find your Majesty. He took it very much upon the huff at last, and rode off swearing hotly that were your Majesty this side o' the water he would unearth you at last. 'His father's blood boiled within him,' quoth he, 'and kept him from sleep,' to think on such a campaign going forward without him," added Sir John, dryly.

The King shrugged his shoulders, with a whimsical twist of countenance.

"My friends are so zealous," said he. "Never monarch had such friends, I do verily believe," and, taking his chin in his hands, his Majesty appeared to muse.

"Well, gentlemen," said he, after a pause,

" we must e'en hazard it, and the event will be as it must. You will take this paper with the three seals, Mr. Langford, to Colonel Penruddock — no, stay! — to Captain Jacobus. 'T is an adventure to fit Jacobus. Tell the Captain what to do with it, but say nothing to Penruddock, nor to any one. Then, if the treasure resolve itself into a mare's-nest, no one will be disappointed, and I 'll warrant Jacobus will not be a loser in the transaction ; while if there are three thousand pounds to be gained, Jacobus is the man for the job. Salisbury, then, is the point of attack ; you are to carry my commands to Colonel Sir John Penruddock and Sir Joseph Wagstaff to march upon Salisbury immediately, and thence advance on London. Or, if it is better in their judgment to make further inroads upon the West-country before approaching London, let them do so. That must depend upon Sir Marmaduke Darcy and the North-countrymen, of whom Rochester will doubtless send us tidings. Now, have you the message perfectly in your mind, Mr. Langford ?"

" Perfectly, sire."

" You will then embark this afternoon upon

the *Saint Gabriel*, — a little ship belonging to
my friend Mr. Francis Mansel, of Lyme Regis ;
and upon landing at that port, ride post to head-
quarters. As to Captain Jacobus — "

" I am to meet the Captain at Lyme, an it
please your Majesty."

" Why, very well, then there is a piece of
business well concluded," said the King, briskly,
with an air of relief, so that I wondered, with
Sir John Mennes, at his Majesty's indifferent
demeanor, when the gain of a kingdom hung in
the balance.

His Majesty then graciously invited Sir John
and myself to a collation, and going before us
into a room below-stairs giving on the garden,
presented us to his host and hostess. The
master of the house was a round, bald-headed
Dutchman, with a benign countenance and
bristling, up-brushed mustachios ; his wife was
an English lady, very grandly dressed and very
demure, to whom his Majesty, methought,
paid somewhat marked attention. When the
cloth was drawn, and my lady, with a courtesy,
gone from the room, we took our wine into the
garden, — a trim enclosure with red and yellow

sanded walks and fantastical patches of tulips guarded by full-blown leaden Cupids with bended bows.

Here the King made me rehearse the tale of my adventures, whereat his Majesty was mighty entertained. So soon as I had come to an end, 't was time for me to start. As I knelt to take my leave, the jovial King — rocking a little on his feet, for the Dutchman's French wine was very potent — took a ribbon from his doublet from which a gold ring depended, and placed it round my neck.

"If time and chance decree that we meet not again, although I hope we may, Mr. Langford, this trinket may remind you of a merry meeting," said the King. "A good voyage to you, sir."

XI

THE FRENCH GENTLEMAN WITH RED HAIR

THE gray of the morning had turned to gold in the afternoon; and upon quitting the King's lodging, accompanied by Sir John Mennes, I walked along the plangent quays between the tall, shining houses and the glittering sea in a glory of sunlight, my head humming with excitement and the wine. The *Saint Gabriel* was a fore-and-aft rigged craft with foremast and mizzen, which lay by the wharf at the King's disposal in case of need; we boarded her, and took order for my passage; and, the master informing us that we could not sail until the ebb two hours hence, Sir John and I went ashore again to pass the time. My companion, I remember, entertained me with many witty and not over-delicate stories, which I forgot so soon as he had uttered them; and it seemed but a few minutes (in my dazed and happy condi-

tion), before I was aboard again, the sails drawing, and Sir John Mennes, perilously near the
quay-edge, waving his plumed hat, and shouting
ribald farewells.

The vessel slipped smoothly through the
water before a soldier's wind ; and I was watching the houses and spires shrinking, until, with
the setting sun flashing upon the windows, the
city looked like a jewelled toy dropped upon the
sandbank, when I became aware that I was not
the only passenger aboard. A tall man in a
slouched hat, a good deal muffled about the neck,
stood by the cook's galley, smoking a cigarro,
the scent of which is extremely nauseating to an
unstable sailor, and first drew my notice. He
was clean-shaven, and tanned as black as a
gipsy, with dark eyes and red hair, — an odd
combination that took my fancy. My gentleman was staring at me, as I at him ; and I
thought it only civil to cross the deck and
salute him.

"Give you good-den, sir," I said, bowing as
well as I could for the ship.

The stranger shook his head, smiled, removed his hat with a large gesture, and said

something in French, of which language I have no skill. There was clearly no more to be done; so with another congee, I left the Frenchman to himself; and the breeze freshening as the sun went down, sickness came heavily upon me, and I went and lay down in my bunk. All that night the pains of hell gat hold upon me, and I lay on my back, groaning, helpless, and in total darkness. It must have been close on midnight, when a last horror came upon me. I felt light cold touches as of fingers, or rats' feet, passing over my face and breast; but I could not lift hand or foot in my defence; and so far gone was I, that I suffered the terror with a kind of indifference. Presently the visitation ceased; and when morning came, and I revived somewhat, I put it down to rats, or a trick of imagination, and thought no more of it. At any rate, if it was the Frenchman, or a thief of any sort, he had taken nothing from my pocket; for the paper with the three seals, and the King's gift were safe where I had placed them.

All that day and night, and the day following, we fled before a favorable wind; but the pitching of that little cock-boat wrought such sore disruption in my inwards that I held no further commerce with the red-haired stranger, and little enough with any one, being glad to roll myself in my cloak, and snatch a dog-sleep in the sun, whenever I felt a little better; but I contracted a violent hatred of the man, for that he would be always smoking his cursed cigarro to windward of me.

Upon the evening of the second day, we moved alongside the Cobb of Lyme (for so the natives name the curving harbor wall), and, taking my valise in hand, I set out directly for Lyme Regis Church, where Captain Jacobus had appointed to meet me. The blunt gray building was plain to see from the Cobb, standing above the stepped roofs of the houses, where they climbed the hill-side, the checkered fields behind, green and brown, rising into the pale sky. At first the solid ground seemed to heave beneath my feet as I walked, but presently subsided somewhat. I was glad to be ashore again, tramping the solid earth, with the breeze from landward blowing country odors in my face. Upon entering the churchyard, I marked

the figure of the Captain perched on a great
square tombstone, gazing out to sea, where was
a conflagration of sunset like the burning of a
city. His back was towards me, and the smoke
of his pipe floated in thin whorls about him.

Treading softly among the long grass and the
graves, I clapped a hand upon his shoulder.

" In the King's name! " I cried.

Jacobus leaped to his feet with an oath, and
attempted instantly to cover his surprise in
hearty greetings.

" I have been," he said when they were
done, " awaiting you in this accursed graveyard
two days and a night, Anthony," and I thought
he looked mighty weary about the eyes ; "all
alone among the dead mariners, till I began to
think I was dead myself without knowing it.
And the wind crying in my ears the while
something I could never put words to ; and the
sea awash below, and the gulls calling and flying close, and looking into my eyes. . . . And
if I fell asleep in the sun there was always a
stirring and a rustling, and when I awoke something gray and thin I could never rightly see
flitting behind the tombs. And in the night

. . . I tell you, boy, I believe the drowned men come up out o' the deep o' nights in troops. Why should they not? Answer me that. Dead is not dead — not as we think. 'Sblood! Anthony, these buried mariners are not dead enough for me," said Jacobus, stamping on the ground so that his spur rang. "Another night, and I should ha' talked with them face to face.''

Of all men in the world I should least have suspected the Captain of a superstitious seizure. He spoke quite simply and quietly, looking gravely at me the while, although a certain terror lay evidently behind his words, and a foolish shiver ran down my back as I listened.

"Why the devil, then," I cried, " do you hold tryst in graveyards? Faith! next time you shall sail the salt seas, and I will abide among the tombs. It may be unhealthy, but, body o' me! 'tis the Garden of Eden compared with the belly of a ship. For God's sake, man, come and dine. I have had no food for two days and nights."

"Why, you look a trifle gaunt and tallowy," observed Jacobus, with a sudden return to his wonted manner. "I can pick a bit myself. Come down to the Blue Garland."

Arm-in-arm we turned our backs upon the bleak shadows of the windy graveyard, and marched down the steep street in the shrewd spring twilight to the principal inn, where Jacobus, quite himself again, ordered everything in the house to be prepared instantly. Then I recounted all that had befallen since we parted. The Captain listened with the most lively attention, interjecting questions and caustic observations.

"Y' have done very well, my son," he observed, when I had concluded. "Ye have made his Majesty your friend, and, mark me, the King will be a trump card presently. We may not win this round, nor the next; but meanwhile, remember, Oliver ripens fast for hell. As to your friend Manning, I like him not, Anthony. He is too sweet and plausible a gentleman; people are not made so. Charlie Stuart did very right to send the seals to me. To-morrow at sun-up, then, I will ride to Colonel Penruddock at Compton Chamberlain, while you strike out for the Hampshire contingent ; both regiments to muster at Salisbury two days hence, on second April."

"Why, the Chief Justice and four judges will be on circuit in the city, now I bethink me," I said.

"So much the worse for them," remarked Jacobus, "and the better for us. 'T will show the country we care naught for rebel administrations. My Lord Protector will be vastly pleased when he hears of his five right worshipful justices all a-row kicking heels in hemp."

We were sitting over our wine by this time ; and although there remained no trace in the Captain's bearing of his singular lapse in the churchyard, yet there lurked something of a question in his glance, a tincture of doubt in his manner. I knew what he would be at ; a man of his mould would sooner be torn in pieces than stoop to explain or to condone his own momentary weakness ; while vanity pricked him to discover whether I thought the less of him for such an exhibition ; and I cast about how to ease his mind.

"You were speaking of spiritual visitations but now," I began, at a pause in the con-

The French Gentleman

versation, and Jacobus looked up suspiciously.
"Well, I do not rate myself a coward, but I
suffered an experience on ship-board that sucked
me out the very dregs of courage. I do not
shame to say it, and yet it was a very trifling
affair, when all's told. I suppose there is no
man ever lived that terror has not gripped his
entrails, at one time or another. Do you not
think so yourself, Captain?"

"Why, yes," said Jacobus, indifferently,
"and what kind of a demon laid his claws upon
you, Anthony?"

I told him of the prying fingers that touched
me when I lay sick and helpless in my berth;
and he said it was a strange thing; and thereupon passed to discussion of our plan of action.
But I noted that he regarded me now with a
restful eye.

It was arranged that if, directly upon my
arrival at Salisbury, Penruddock's force held the
city, I should proceed to the house of Mayor
Phelps; and that if Jacobus were not there, I
should seek him in the Beggars' Chapel in
Grovely Wood. If Penruddock had not arrived before me, I was still to proceed to

Mayor Phelps's where, if I did not find the Captain, I was to await him. Jacobus had brought my gray gelding, the gift of pretty Mrs. Beatrix, and stabled him with his own horse. The mention of the nags reminded him that we should go and see how they did before we went to bed; and he hallo'd for a lantern. The landlord, a blue-faced, corpulous person, brought it himself.

"Does this gentleman sleep here, to-night, sir?" he inquired of the Captain.

"What do you mean by that?" returned Jacobus, sharply. "Did I not bespeak a room for Mr. Langford three days agone?"

"Mr. Langford," said the man, staring angrily at me. "Which is Mr. Langford, then? Are there two Mr. Langfords? Or have I been made a fool of?"

"Go to," said Jacobus. "Y' are drunk. This is Mr. Langford, sot. What the devil are you talking about?"

A ridiculous bewilderment crept upon the landlord's shaggy visage. "Why, then, I have been made a fool," said he, helplessly. "And the nag gone too. As God's-my-life,

't was no fault of mine, sirs. The gentleman
looked a gentleman, sure enough, and——"

"Just tell the story, if you please," said
Jacobus, sternly. He was sitting upon the table,
swinging a leg, according to his habit. The
bulky landlord stood quaking before him like
a school-boy at fault, the great horn stable-
lantern, smokily alight, dangling from his finger.

"I am telling you, sir," said the miserable
man. "'T was just this way, sirs," looking
appealingly at me, —— "just this way, as I was
saying. Just about sun-down — ay, scarce a
half-an-hour afore ye come in yourselves, sirs —
in marches a great gentleman hot-foot. 'Has
a gentleman left a horse here for Mr. Langford?'
says he. 'Are you Mr. Langford?' I asked
of him, and he stares at me fierce. 'Of course,'
he says. 'My service to you, sir,' I says, 'Mr.
Simeon' [the name the Captain had adopted for
the nonce] 'brought a led horse along wi' him,
't is in stable now. Belike 't is the nag your
honor means.' 'What is the beast like?' he
asked. 'A gray gelding,' I tells him. 'That's
my horse,' quo' he. 'Saddle him quick 's you
can. Mr. Simeon is awaiting me, is he not,'

says he. 'Surely,' I says, 'and I expect him to come in every next moment,' says I, 'for 's dinner.' 'Do you so?' says he, 'well, 't is a mighty pity I cannot wait. Present my compliments to Mr. Simeon, and belike he and I will meet in Salisbury,' says he, and by that time the gelding was brought round, and my gentleman tosses Tom ostler a crown, vaults into saddle, drives spurs in, and off at a cruel hard gallop over t' cobbles."

I broke into a laugh as the man paused with dropped jaw, gazing timorously at Jacobus, who was gnawing his moustachios.

"And why did you not tell me all this before, sirrah?" demanded the Captain, so fiercely that the man gave back a step.

"God forgive me," he whined, "it went clean out o' my head."

"What was the man like? Describe him!" said Jacobus.

"I marked not what he wore," said the man, "but a' had black eyes and red hair, I will swear to 't."

I exclaimed in surprise, but the Captain went on without a pause.

The French Gentleman

"Look you, dolt," said he, "you tell me there is a nag of mine gone from your stables; well, then, you must make good the loss, and that before to-morrow morning. I have no more to say than that," and getting leisurely from the table, Jacobus turned his back to the culprit, and spread his fingers to the fire.

"Come now, y' are unreasonable, Mr. Simeon," said the landlord, sullenly. "'T is all as I have told you. 'T was no fault o' mine. Anything I can do to convenience the gentleman I will, such as lending him a mount for a stage or so. But to buy another nag — and 'twixt now and sun-up! It can't be done, sirs, and more," he added, encouraged by his own words, "I will not do 't. How do I know the red-haired gentleman and yourself are not acquaint?"

I do not know whether the Captain, finding his will opposed, acted merely from force of habit, forgetting his disguise — for he was posing as Mr. Gabriel Simeon, wool-stapler — or whether his passion for effect overcame all other considerations. However it was, at the inn-keeper's last words he turned sharply upon him, lugging out a pistol, and levelled it at his head.

"Take the door, Anthony," said Jacobus; and I crossed the room and leaned against the panel. I was thus behind the landlord, so that he could not see me wrestling with laughter.

"Now then, Master Nick-and-Froth," went on the Captain, falling into his professional manner, "I have no time to waste, and (if you will believe me) no more have you. Half-a-minute is not a long time wherein to make ready for death, is it?—especially for a man of your habits. And yet, sirrah, 't is all you possess unless you give me an undertaking to furnish me a good nag before sunrise. I will take forty broad pieces for a bond, meanwhile. Come! I will count the seconds for you: One, two!—"

"Sirs! sirs!" cried the man, "will ye do murder?"—and I could see the water start and glisten on his temple.

"Seven, eight, nine, ten! One moment, Innkeeper. Y' are thinking I would not dare to shoot you. Do not so deceive yourself. Let me tell you, my friend, that I am a King's man, while you, I take it, are a bloody Round-head, and I would make no more of killing you than you would of sticking a pig. To resume : Eleven, twelve," and Jacobus counted up to twenty-five, cocking his pistol on the word, when the fellow cried out, with a high, strang-ling vociferation : —

"I will do it," he said ; and as the Captain lowered his weapon, sobbed out a stream of curses.

"'T is like the letting of blood — it relieves the heart and veins, and I make a rule to allow it," observed Jacobus to me, as if in apology. "Now I will take the forty pieces, if you please," said he, advancing towards the inn-keeper.

The light ran coldly down the pistol-barrel ; the man turned with an obedient start, and, still carrying the lantern, shambled before us into his private den, where he counted out the money in a sullen silence.

The Captain repaid him the amount of the reckoning, and, after seeing that the Captain's horse was cared for, we sat down to finish the bottle.

"The scurvy rogue," said Jacobus; "'t is amazing how few persons can perceive their manifest obligations save in the throat of a pistol-barrel. And what do you think of our red-haired horse-monger, Mr. Langford?"

"I think his name is Manning," I said, rather shamefacedly.

"O! do you so?" cried Jacobus. "Y' have a most uncommon penetration. I make you my compliments."

"You are to remember," I expostulated, "that the first time I saw him I had but just come from his Majesty's table; and the rest of the voyage I was sick as a dog."

"You were disguised in liquor and he was disguised in a wig, as it were," said the Captain, grinning at his jest. "Now I will read ye your ghostly riddle, Mr. Langford. The spirit's name was Manning too; and Manning picked your pockets to see if you had the three seals. Manning is brewing a plot, boy, and doubtless thinks himself mighty clever at it. Well, I will have my spoon in the broth before all's done. And if you had but quietly put your iron through the gentleman upon a certain occasion, ye had saved a world of trouble. For a youth of parts, I sometimes think y' are a fool, Anthony."

Indeed, I thought so too. Manning had outwitted me, and was even now galloping to Salisbury upon no one knew what devil's errand; and I believed him capable of the worst crimes. 'T was doubtless his face I saw at the window of the inn 'twixt Flushing and Middleburgh; he had tracked me like a dog, and, dolt that I was, I could have stabbed myself.

"Let us start to-night, for God's sake, Captain," I said; but Jacobus would not hear of it.

"You do not know what is in front of you, lad. Sleep you must, or you cannot go through with it. Y' are thinking of the girl, I know very well; but content you, she hath her father, hath she not? At any rate, we could never overtake the man. Besides, y' have no horse. A lover's imagination is ever prophesying evil falsely. Go to bed and to sleep, man."

And so I did; for since we could not ride, I found myself deadly wearied.

XII

I TAKE THE ROAD UPON MY OWN ACCOUNT

SURE enough, next morning the ostler brought to the door a handsome roan mare, fully equipped. Upon putting her through her paces and looking her over, Jacobus and I, both professed horse-copers, found her to all appearance sound; and after returning the amount of his bond to the landlord, we set forth. We rode along the coast together so far as Charmouth, where our roads parted; Jacobus travelling northeast by Sherborne and Frome to Compton Chamberlayn, in Wiltshire, while my route lay further south through Bridport, Dorchester, Blandford, and Cranborne Chase to Fordingbridge, in Hampshire, where dwelt Mr. William Jenkins, Captain of the Hampshire contingent. Jacobus had near upon seven

leagues further to ride than I, while Compton
Chamberlayn lay three hours further from Salisbury, where both regiments were to muster at
five in the morning of April the second, than
Fordingbridge; but the Captain reckoned by
means of incessant riding, frequent change of
horses, and his knowledge of the country, to
accomplish his journey in the time. The
allowance of another day could have caused no
jot of harm; while (as events fell out) the
time gained might have saved many a loyal life.
But the Captain was never content, unless he
were doing just a little trifle more than any
other man was satisfied in accomplishing.

After I had parted from Jacobus, the mare
stumbled badly twice or thrice during the next
few miles, but I thought little of it, rode easy,
and stopped at Bridport to bait her and to
drink a tankard of October. By the time we
were well out on the Dorset Downs, under the
shoulder of Shipton Beacon, the nag began to
trip again; I dismounted, and examined her
hocks, which were swollen and tender, and
which must have been bandaged for a week
before to have reduced them to the normal

condition in which they seemed that morning. There was nothing for it but to push on ; and on we went. But presently, going down hill, the mare stumbled again and fell heavily, pitching me into the road. I came down upon my head, which seemed to explode like a shell at the concussion. I do not know how long I lay there ; but when I sat up the ground heaved in billows, the sky was dark and rained stars. After drinking a little Hollands from my flask I felt better, though my head ached infernally, and my right arm was bruised and swollen from shoulder to elbow. Coming a little more to myself, a horrible pang seized me ; I staggered to my feet and looked round.

There was no mare to be seen ; she was clean gone, with forty broad pieces in the saddle-bags, and my pistols — Manning's pistols — in the holsters. Doubtless that devilish nag was far on the road to Lyme by now. Mine host of the Blue Garland was avenged. I was sick as a dog, and every bone rebelled ; but the urgency of my errand burned within me, and, hardly knowing what I did, I set my face to the east and began to plod forward. My

mind grew clearer as I walked, and I began to
consider the situation. A horse I must have;
for, although 't was barely possible to tramp
the distance in the time, a mistake in the direc-
tion, or a few hours' rain (for already the
roads were soft), would defeat me, and I dared
not risk it. Searching my pockets, I found (I
remember accurately) three Jacobuses, a crown,
seven shillings, and a groat. Certainly I could
not buy a horse with those remunerations.

When necessity sets the grip upon a man,
't is wonderful how it changes his opinion of
the Ten Commandments. He perceives in a
wink the margin of that absolute document,
close written with a great number of valuable
saving clauses, hitherto unnoted. And, after
trudging valley and upland for some three hours,
I had resolved, like iron, the first reasonable
good nag I met should somehow change owners.

'T was already falling dusk on those desolate
wolds when I was aware of a horseman approaching on a bright bay stallion. As he drew
near, I hailed him.

"Give you good-den, sir," I said; "I
would have a word with you."

Seeing, I suppose, that I had not the air of a common foot-pad, the man drew rein — without, however, giving himself the trouble to return my salutation. He was a big, sulky-looking farmer fellow, plainly clad in gray homespun, with an uphill nose and a monstrous jowl like a bull-dog, and he carried a stout holly staff.

"Will you sell me your horse?"

"I will not, certainly," he returned in surly accents. "Is that all you wanted? Out o' my way!"

I caught his bridle with my left hand. "Sir," I said, "I am about an errand of life and death. A horse I must have. What is your price?"

He considered a moment. "Forty broad pieces, down on the nail," said he.

"Meet me at the Poultry Cross in Salisbury the day after to-morrow, and I will give you sixty."

"Belike!" said the farmer, his great face flushing. "And who are you, my fine sir, with the bloody coxcomb?"

"That is my business," quoth I.

"I can tell thee, nevertheless. Thou 'rt a mountebank tricked up, or a ruffling bloody Cavalier " — and I saw that he had cropped his locks, which a Royalist yeoman would not do. "Take hand from my rein, man, or I will break the rest o' thy head for thee. Snick up!"

He raised his cudgel; I drew a dag[1] from my belt, grasping it by the barrel, for 't was unloaded. For a moment we watched each other warily; then my yeoman struck at me, at the same time spurring his horse, which reared, for I held the bridle fast. With a quick motion of the head I avoided his blow, which fell upon my left shoulder, that was defended by the leather pauldron of my buff coat, and I brought down the pistol-butt upon my antagonist's right wrist with all the force I could muster in my maimed arm. The stroke rang as though I had beaten a billet of wood to flinders, and the man dropped his cudgel with a snarl like a baited bear. Still holding the rein, I stooped swiftly to pick it up, and the plunging of the frightened nag gave me enough to do to reach it. As I rose with the staff in my hand, the farmer

[1] A small pistol.

caught me a swinging buffet on the side of the head. I was near stunned, and lost control of my anger. You are to remember that while the nag meant no more than salable horse-flesh to the churl, it meant the world to me. I struck at the rider's head. He warded the blow with his left arm; I beat it down, and brought the holly with a goodly thwack upon his pate. The big man swayed sideways and fell bodily upon me, bearing me to the ground. 'T was all I could do to loose his boots from the stirrups and to prevent the nag kicking us both to death. So soon as I had quieted the horse, I bent over the prostrate yeoman and explored his head. The skull was whole, so doubtless he would recover; and, settling him in as easy a posture as I could, I mounted the bay and spurred forward.

By this time the sun had vanished, and white mists crawled in the valleys; and presently I saw the lights of Dorchester town twinkling through the haze. Fearing lest a hue-and-cry should be raised before morning, I avoided the town and pushed on through the gathering darkness. The day's misadventures began to press sore upon me : red-hot hammers beat within my head ; my arm ached to agony from the violence I had used ; and I heard strange sounds and beheld flitting visions of strange sights. Sometimes I would hear bells chiming, and methought they were the bells of Salisbury and I was riding thither ; then I would see Barbara in a room alone with Manning in his red hair, and hear her cry aloud for help. At that I would start to my senses, gather up the reins, and stare into the dark ; then again dreams and stupor would steal upon me. I seemed to have been riding in pain and darkness since the day I was born ; when at last my trusty nag ambled into a village nestling at the base of a great hill, and called, as I learned in the morning, Troy Town. The lighted windows aroused me, and I had sense enough to steer into the stable-yard of the Inn, where I had no sooner dismounted, than I swooned upon the stones. The people of the house must have carried me within-doors and hapt me up in bed : for there I was when I awoke, with a comely white-haired old dame bathing my temples. She gave me something mighty comforting to drink, and bade me to sleep; whereupon I sank straight-way into a dreamless slumber.

'T was broad daylight when I woke again, feeling stiff and sore indeed, but well enough and mighty hungry — so potent a medicament is youth. When I appeared downstairs my hostess cried out as though I had been a ghost, and would have it I must to bed again. But upon beholding the breakfast I consumed, she thought better of it, and after bandaging my head and arm afresh with some wonderful decoction of herbs and simples, and reiterating a hundred wise cautions, she let me go. My hostess of Troy Town tavern was a kindly, winsome old lady, in her clean lilac gown and great white cap; one of those whose simple nature is all to do good to others; and who, methinks, in this rude world's march, are too often shoved aside and trampled on.

The nag I had won by force of arms was a good nag, strong, steady, and handsome; and in the saddle-bags I found thirty-three broad pieces, some loose silver and copper, three little soiled linen bags containing samples of corn and a new whip-lash. My friend the Roundhead yeoman must have prospered in Dorchester market the day before. As for me, now I came to think of it by morning light, I had committed a common highway robbery; there was the plain fact. Anthony Langford of Langford Manor was no better than a thief and a robber.

Hitherto I had regarded my friend Captain Jacobus with a moral reservation; he was this and that, and 't was excellent well, but there was a flaw in the crystal of his honor. Now I began to perceive he entertained precisely that opinion of myself; and (it appeared) with the better reason, and the greater forbearance. I recalled my heady speech the day we halted above Winchester city, glittering beneath us in the valley. I thought myself something heroical at the time, and yet I had but figured as a pragmatical whipster blown up with swelling conceits. Well, there seemed no certitude in morals, and for the first time it began to dawn upon my raw intelligence that life is not a routine to be smoothly undertaken by the aid of maxims, as your cook by recipe makes kickshaws and pigeon-pasty, but a delicate, chancy business requiring an alert habit of diplomacy.

Captain Jacobus

My luck was surely out for the time; for a thick rain and mist driving before an east wind soaked me to the skin; there was no sun to steer by; and the road, at best a mere cart-rut, perplexed me continually by its divergences. So it was that after riding endlong over hill and heath all day, I came at dusk upon a desolate table-land where the wind blew salt, and the fog, rolling clear, unveiled a great plain of waters beyond the trending coast-line some two miles distant. Nearer hand, beside the sullen gleam of a river, the wet roofs of a town shone in the fading light. I had travelled in a circle and come to the sea again. There was nothing for it but to go down into the town and lodge there for the night. I found the place to be Wareham, near by Poole Harbor, and thus, instead of arriving at Fordingbridge as I had reckoned, I was still, upon a reasonable near guess, some thirty miles distant. Moreover, the nag was wearied out, and I myself could no longer sit upright in the saddle. The Hampshire troop would be late at the muster, for all I could do; 't was the woundiest hinderance, but the lot I must bear, in spite of my teeth.

I take the Road

Next morning I was on the road again long ere sunrise, taking the ostler of mine Inn to guide me so far as Woolbridge; and so I arrived at Fordingbridge and the house of Mr. Will Jenkins at ten in the forenoon, five hours after the whole troop should have kept tryst at Salisbury. Mr. Jenkins despatched half-a-dozen riders hot-foot to the gentlemen concerned in the conspiracy, who were billeted with their followers in the manor and farm-houses of the neighborhood; while his wife and a bevy of comely daughters made me great cheer, pressing to stay and be healed of my bruises, or at least to await the riding of the troop. But I had scarce patience to eat some bread and meat, and drink a stoup of wine; and borrowing a fresh horse, I struck spurs in and rode off at top speed for Salisbury.

XIII

HOW THE ROYALISTS OCCUPIED SALISBURY TOWN

MY road lay along the familiar banks of Avon, and through my own estate and village of Langford. As I rode up the street the desperate clatter of hoofs brought women to their cottage-doors; and more than one fellow, recognizing me, waved his cap and cried out a greeting.

A wild clangor of bells came faintly down wind; and coming in sight of Salisbury Cathedral, pale against the lowering gray sky, I discerned, above the battlement where the steeple springs from the tower, a black speck like a fly crawl out upon the yellow stonework, and unfurl a speckle of gold and scarlet that twinkled in the wind. Methought I saw a pygmy arm flung up (no bigger than a bristle), and I knew

194

the man was cheering the Royal Standard. The city was won, then. A frenzy of excitement seized me; I remember rising in my stirrups, waving my hat and holloing till the wood and water rang. The pealing clamor of the great bells swelled momently louder until the whole air was filled with clashing tintinabulations; and presently horse and man galloped across the Chapel Bridge where John Manning had lain in ambush for me, and where (curse him) I had let him go free.

The city was in a mighty turmoil. The houses seemed to have emptied into the streets, which were thronged with a shouting tide of cits, shopmen, 'prentices, and idle fellows, setting towards the Market Place. Here and there a Royalist trooper in steel cap, back and breast, with a couple or more led horses jibbing at his elbow (conveyed without doubt from the nearest stable) would be thrusting his way through the press with oaths and the butt of his arquebus. Not a shop was open, and many of them were being fortified and barricadoed by the fat burgesses and greasy tradesfolk with doors wrenched off their hinges, floor-boards, and ends of timber.

They sweated at the work like men possessed; so hot was their hurry that (although I noted it not at the time) I recollect my memory of one such engineer, his puffy face all crimson, who, smiting at tenpenny nails with a great hammer, struck his fingers till a red stain came out upon the white wood, yet he never blenched nor paused.

Across the top of the High Street, at its entrance into the Market-place, a double file of cavalry was posted to keep the mobile back. Upon giving the word, "A Roland," one returned the counter, "For Oliver," the ranks opened, closed behind me, and I found myself in the Market-place. A squadron of cavalry was drawn up in the form of a hollow square, in the midst of which stood a knot of gentlemen on horseback conferring together, amongst whom I perceived Sir John Penruddock and Sir Joseph Wagstaff. Except for the troopers, the Market-place was empty, files being stationed at the entering in of the streets. The windows of all the houses were white with faces and alive with gazing eyes; the roofs and gables were moving with spectators; a gray, still sky brooded over all, so that the motley of colors were singularly distinct, and save for the incessant tumult of the bells overhead, there reigned an ominous silence. I would have pushed through the horsemen to Sir John Penruddock, to inform him of the speedy arrival of the Hampshire troop; but a major near by, hearing a commotion, turned with an oath and commanded order; and at that moment the ranks on the further side of the square opened out, I caught a flash of moving scarlet, and the two judges, in their robes of red trimmed with ermine, and the sheriff in his furred gown, marched into the midst of the Market-place, conducted by a couple of troopers on either hand with swords drawn, and halted in front of the group of gentlemen. Sir Joseph Wagstaff put his horse a pace forward, and made a speech, of which I could only catch a word here and there. But the pealing of the bells suddenly ceasing, he raised his voice, so that the words echoed.

"And so, my lords, and you, Mr. Sheriff, are condemned by the King his Majesty, against whom y' are taken in rebellion, seditiously administering rebel ordinances upon the bodies of his loyal and faithful subjects, to be hanged by the neck until ye be dead, and may God have mercy on your souls."

He ceased, and a kind of tremor ran through the multitude. Then the Lord Chief Justice Rolles stepped forward, with his parchment of commission unfurled in his hand, and began to speak. I could not hear his words; but before he had done, Sir John Penruddock spurred up to Sir Joseph Wagstaff, and rounded him eagerly in the ear. The rest of the gentlemen crowded round, and they conversed together, the two bearded men in scarlet looking quietly on, with no sign of trepidation. In a little Sir John Penruddock put his horse toward them, and cried out in a great voice, —

"My lords, upon due consideration of your plea for mercy, ye are reprieved for this time. For you, Mr. Sheriff, y' are arrested."

The sheriff, who was standing a little back, hurried forward and fell on his knees before the knight, with clasped hands upraised, crying aloud for mercy in a weeping voice.

"God-'a-mercy, Sir John," cried one of the gentlemen, "hang all or none! Truss up the pitiful knave, and bring him along for a hostage.''

At a word from Sir Joseph two of the troopers who had been guarding the judges took the wretched sheriff by the elbows, jerked him to his feet, and bound his arms behind him. I heard the men round me swearing freely. "This is no way to set about the business," quoth one, "to condemn one minute and pardon the next." And, indeed, I was much of the same opinion.

The judges, after exchanging a few words with the officers, delivered up their commissions and turned to depart, the gentlemen raising their hats to them, and the ranks opening out again to let them through. The people at the windows and upon the house-tops set up a great shout, but whether for joy or anger I could not tell. As the troops began to move and to re-form I spurred through the press to Sir John Penruddock.

"Mr. Langford, I think," said he, saluting me. "Where are the Hampshiremen, sir?"

I explained the delay as best I could, but he scarce heard me out.

" 'T is no matter," he said. " We have done very well without them, you see. The city surrendered at discretion. We march down West, whither they may follow at their leisure. Give you good-den, Mr. Langford," and, raising his hat, he turned away. Sir John was plainly a good deal elated, but (had he only known it) no man had ever less reason in this world.

Making my way to the Poultry Cross, I gave my horse to a trooper, and, with beating heart, went up to the door of Mayor Phelps's house. I knocked in vain, and finding the door upon the latch, I entered the hall. Methought as I crossed the threshold that I heard a noise of hammering, as of some one cleaving wood; but no sooner had I closed the door behind me than the sound ceased. I stood quiet and listened; there was nothing to be heard save the tick-tack of the tall clock in the corner. I hurried from room to room, but all were empty; the door of Barbara's chamber stood open, and I went in softly, with a sense of profanation. 'T was all in confusion, cupboards and chests standing open, clothes and dainty gear tossed upon the bed and upon the floor, where I spied a pair of tiny, red-heeled shoon, and put them in my pocket. Pausing to weigh this strange condition of affairs, I heard the knocking sounds re-commence downstairs. I descended swiftly to the hall, but before I had reached the stair-foot all was once more still.

The hall was a long, sombre room, with a wide, diamond-paned window looking on the street at one end, and a massive staircase ascending at the other. Dim portraits of men in armor, and demure ladies in ruff and stomacher (for the Phelpses came of a good lineage) were framed in the brown panelling that lined the walls from oaken floor to oak-beamed ceiling. As I stood gazing in absence of mind at the profile of a helmed warrior whose picture was next to the great stone fireplace, I suddenly beheld his eyeball move, a shining speck in the gloom. My skin crept upon me, and I glanced fearfully round at the shadows that lurked in the corners; then I looked again. The dead Elizabethan was gazing in front of him under painted lids. My brain was tricking me again, I supposed; and small wonder, for my battered head ached sorely whenever I had time to think about it. I drew a step nearer, staring at the picture; when my heart gave a bursting leap, for a voice issued from the wall.

"I fear I must put you to the trouble of releasing me, Mr. Langford," it said, in muffled tones. "Touch the spring, and undo the bolts, if you please."

I had no notion there was a secret chamber, or priest's hole, in that place; and marvelling greatly, sought for the spring. The voice continued to direct me; and at length a massy steel lever shot back, the whole picture opened outwards like a door, and who should step over the wainscot but Manning, with his high look and superior air, and neatly tied love-lock, just as I had last beheld him under that roof.

"Give you good-den, Mr. Langford," said he, politely. "I am sorry to have put you to so much trouble. But I made no doubt you knew the secrets of this house at least so well as I," said Manning, with sarcasm.

There were a good many questions which I should have liked Manning to resolve for me: Had he aught to do with the deprivation of my estate, and what was the Plymouth Plot? Why had he spied upon me from the window of the inn among the Flemish sand-dunes? Why had he pried into my pockets that night upon the *Saint Gabriel,* masquerading in the French language and a wig? Why had he stolen my horse from the Blue Garland? How dared he? Where were the three seals, and the three thousand pounds? And where Jacobus? Above all, where was Barbara? Why was the house empty, while he was bolted into the priest's hole? And again, what the devil was he doing there, after my warning, and challenge on the Chapel Bridge?

Manning stood gazing insolently at me, hand on hip, as I ran these things over in my mind; and looking at him, it came upon me that the only proposition in the world I could make to such a fellow was the last on the catalogue. I accordingly propounded it; and so it was that I never got solutions to any of my problems from Manning.

"My privy business, I have the honor to presume," answered Manning.

"Well, you remember what I told you?" said I.   203

"I recollect me perfectly of your singular courtesy," returned Manning. "'Sblood, how much longer will you dilly-dally about this business?" he shouted, in sudden insane fury. "Must I spit in your face, you dog, to make you fight?" and therewith he caught me a buffet on my wounded head, that struck like a bolt of fire.

Half blinded with the pain, I drew upon him; our rapiers hissed from the scabbards at the same instant; and we set-to like a couple of bulls. I used both hands, to ease my maimed arm that was mighty sore and stiff, holding the blade just over the hilts with my left gauntlet, as one does at the end of a long fencing bout. Manning fought with the light of the window in his eyes, so that I had a small advantage; and my arm growing easier and my head clearer, I began to press him hard. The sweat glistened on his forehead, and he panted aloud; but he was a stanch fighter, full as good at tricks of fence as I, and in far better trim; and I began to wonder how long I could hold out. I had pricked him once or twice, and my foot had near slipped in my own blood; the sparks were flying, and the room ringing like a stithy, when a door clapped, and in another moment our blades were stricken up by old Richard Phelps, with a half-pike he must have snatched from the wall as he entered. Instantly Manning slipped behind the Mayor, and ran out of the house, slamming the door in my face. Next moment I was out and after him, to see him with a dash of his sword cut down the trooper who held my horse, leap upon the nag's back, drive spurs in, and away, the people running this way and that at the rattle of the hoofs. Pursuing him hot-foot, the bloody rapier naked in my hand, I kept him in sight until we cleared the streets, where troopers were still straggling out after Sir John Penruddock's main body. But I was already spent; and scarce a bow-shoot from the walls, I was fain to stop and lean upon my sword for breath. In a pater-noster-while, a big dragoon with a couple of led horses in his fist, drew rein beside me.

"What, man! Hast been in a fray, and gotten the worst o't, by'r Lady. Art for Cæsar? What will ye give me for Roland, then?"

Captain Jacobus

" Oliver," I said, gasping.

" Right so. Why, then, get astride the nag."

I laid hold of the animal, but had not the trooper dismounted to help me, I could not have climbed upon his back. We rode together to Wilton, where we halted at the Orle of Martlets. Giving the man a crown to drink my health, he brought me out a tasse of wine, which revived me somewhat, and I rode on alone into Grovely Wood, where by good fortune I stumbled upon the track to the thieves' chapel. By this time I was become so horribly ill that methought I should never live to get there, and rode in agony, lying on my horse's neck. As we came out upon the clearing where stood the chapel, I beheld the figure of Barbara standing on the threshold, and heard her voice, and saw her run towards me, and rolled senseless at her feet.

XIV

HOW CAPTAIN JACOBUS EXECUTED THE KING'S COMMISSION

'TWAS a week since the capture of the city. I was basking in the sun on mattress and pillows, on the grass outside the Beggars' Chapel, occupying the very place of one of those sentries whom Jacobus and I, little more than three weeks agone, had found asleep, his match smouldering beside him; while the Captain himself lay in the place of the other rascal, smoking a cigarro, his hat over his eyes; and Barbara sat above me in an orange-tawny velvet chair. At a little distance, beyond the bubbling stream, stood the covered wagon of the half-dozen Egyptians whom the Captain had retained for servants; the swarthy people in their bright garments were gathered about a crackling wood fire, above which, amid the curling blue smoke, hung a pot upon a tripod.

Beyond, the forest closed us in, dressed in its spring bravery; between the rough trunks, hyacinths hid the ground like a blue mist; overhead, fragile, tiny clouds voyaged upon the blue before a westerly gale; while now and again the jolly sun would veil his face behind the mounded purple wrack.

The Captain had dispersed the rest of the beggars and gypsies north, east, south, and west; had caused the chapel to be cleansed from floor to roof-tree, and to be strewn with fresh rushes; had transformed his room of the sacristy into a sleeping-chamber for Barbara and her nurse; and had built a partition of branches in the body of the place for my benefit; while Jacobus himself commonly watched me by night, and slept as he could by day. He had gone down to Salisbury upon the night of my arrival, and informed Mr. Phelps of matters; the old man had ridden up twice or thrice, laden with cordials and dainties for the sick man; but Barbara had declined to return with her father, or to admit an apothecary; saying that her business was to nurse me until I was whole, and that she was a better doctor than

any barber-surgeon of them all. Meanwhile,
for the last three days, I had slept almost con-
tinuously; and now, as I lay in the blessed
sunlight, save for a certain languor and stiffness,
I felt a whole man once more. Therefore, I
requested the dozing Captain to give me the
news, and a full relation of his adventures
in the house of Mayor Phelps. Jacobus con-
sulted my physician with a look, who nodded
permission.

"Fair and softly, boy," said he; "what
made you a day late at Fordingbridge?"

"I lost my horse first, then my head, and
last my way," I replied.

"All that?" remarked Jacobus. "Well,
you found your way again, I take it, and you
seem to have regained a kind of headpiece, if
a little the worse for wear. But how did you
get a horse? Or did you walk? Y' had time
enough?"

The Captain's tone was scarcely flattering;
but put it every way I had not shone in my
exploits, and 't was foolish to take offence.

"There are plenty of nags upon the road,"
I said, mildly.

Jacobus did not move so much as an eyelid. There was an appreciable pause, and when he spoke, requesting me to tell my story, he did not betray the slightest sense of what was implied by my admission. I briefly related my misfortunes. When I came to Manning's escape, Jacobus swore blasphemously until he caught the look upon Mrs. Barbara's face.

"I crave your pardon, mistress," said he; "but I left the man for Anthony to kill, and he 's let him go. I would 'a' cut his throat else."

"I do not like such talk," said Barbara, soberly.

"What of Penruddock?" I asked, for neither had I any great desire to discuss Mr. Manning.

"Colonel Penruddock and the best part of his troop are lodged in Exeter Jail," said Jacobus, evenly.

"What!" I cried. "Is the plot at an end, then?" My gilded expectations trembled like a house of cards.

"Plot!" returned Jacobus, savagely, "'t was a schoolboy's freak — 't was the King of France with forty thousand men — 't was anything you

please. Colonel John and Major Joseph, with not
forty hundred, — not four hundred, as God 's my
life, — go out to conquer a kingdom of soldiers !
They take Salisbury without a blow struck on
either side ; and had they laid down any sort
of plan whatsoever — had they even waited for
your damned Hampshiremen, or marched on
London, things might have gone better ; the
country might have taken fire, and at any rate
nothing could have fallen out worse. But,
having captured the city by five in the morning,
they desert it by two in the afternoon, without
leaving so much as a corporal's guard for garri-
son. They do not even hang the bloody judges.
Whereupon all things resume their course as
though the soldiers had never set foot in the
town. Why did they so at all ? What, 'a
God's name, did they think they were doing !
Well, as I say, Sir John and Sir Joseph sound
tuckets, march away down west towards Blandford with drums beating and colors flying for
some two or three hours, when who should they
meet but our old friend Captain Crook with his
patrol of dragoons. The Royalist horses were
wearied out, the army could neither fight nor fly ;

whereupon Crook promises free pardon on the word of a gentleman to all who yield peaceably ; and the end of it was that Sir John and the most of them gave up their arms, while Sir Joseph and the rest, having, I suppose, some glimmerings of sense, got away on foot into hiding. Next day Crook drives the whole posse like sheep into Exeter Jail, where they are now awaiting the butcher. The Hampshire gentlemen, finding Salisbury empty, swept, and garnished, rode quietly home again, like wise men. So ends the Penruddock Plot for the glorious restoration of our sovereign lord the king," Jacobus ended, getting up and striding across the grass to relight his cigarro at the gypsies' fire.

Barbara laid her hand on mine for a moment. For myself I had scant reason to complain, but I was dreadfully oppressed.

"They will not dare to hang them ? " I said, when Jacobus returned.

"Will they not ? " said he. "Is there any horrible crime Oliver will shirk ? And these men were taken red-handed in rebellion. A promise ! What is a promise to a Puritan ?

They have changed the code of gentlemen for
the Book of Leviticus.''

The rarity seemed to have gone out of the
sunshine, and we sat in silence. Presently
Jacobus, perhaps to divert my thoughts, took
up the tale of his adventures.

"We entered the city about five of the clock
on the morning of April 2d, as I have said,
a troop of horse about two hundred strong, all
as arranged. First we rode to the jail, and
threatened to carry the place by assault unless
they opened the gates, which they did. Whereupon we entered and turned all the prisoners
loose into the streets. Some of my own beggar-
spies were among 'em. Then we dispersed in
bands to requisition all the horses in the town.
I took a hand in that also, and 't was excellent
sport. These little risings fail invariably, but
they are admirable fooling while they last. After
that I went to breakfast with the officers at the
sign of the Sun over against the Conduit, where
master inn-keeper could find naught good enough
to set before us; I never beheld a man so instantly obsequious. Before we had done there
comes one running to say that the Mayor and

Aldermen were assembled in the Town Hall, whither the Colonel and Sir Joseph went immediately. I stayed till I had finished breakfast, when I thought it a suitable time to present the paper of seals at the house of Mayor Phelps, so rode leisurely up High Street and across the Market-place. All the troopers — gentlemen, yeomen, and churls — were carousing on every side; the cits welcomed 'em like brothers; and ale was flowing like a festival. A parcel of madcaps had set the bells going; altogether, 't was like the capture of a city in a play-house. I had my own affairs to mind, or, body o' me, I would have shown the Colonel another-guess way to set about the business.

"Well, I left my horse with the soberest soldado I could see, found the house, and knocked upon the panel. 'T was opened at once by a tall, black-avised gallant, whom I surmised to be Manning himself, as I had expected.

"'Give you good-den, Mr. Manning,' I said, to make sure.

"'Y' have my name very pat,' said he. 'I have not the honor of knowing you, I think.'

"'Here is that may serve for recommendation,' I said, and showed him the paper of seals.

" He put out his hand to take it, but I stowed it back in my pocket.

" ' Come in, sir, and welcome,' said he, and led me into a little business-looking cabinet at the back of the hall, and shut the door. There was a leash of tankards on the table, and after pledging each other, we sat down. For all his easy manner, I could see that the fellow suspected me bitterly, fearing, I suppose, that you had penetrated his disguise, and had informed me of his doings.

" ' Is not your name Simeon, sir ? ' said Mr. Manning, looking at me.

" ' Why, no,' I said. ' My name is Jacobus, Captain Jacobus. You have never heard it before, perhaps ? '

" ' Indeed,' says my gentleman, with a bow, ' 't is a title I have long been familiar with. But y' are a little trifle like a certain Mr. Simeon I did once know, at the first glance. Well, I have three thousand pounds to deliver to you, sir ; and I am glad to confide the moneys to such experienced hands,' says he. ' But prithee, Captain, how go matters in the town ? '

"I shrugged my shoulders and pulled a long face, for I wanted to see what he would be at.

" 'Well enough,' I said. ' 'T is not very difficult to march a troop of horse into an unarmed country place.'

" 'You think, then, the event is doubtful,' he asked.

" 'Come,' I returned, 'you and I, dear sir, are men of the great world. We are about a matter of some moment, and I will be open with you. Is it probable that a handful of raw cavalry can upset a kingdom guarded by the finest army in the world ? '

"Mr. Manning was visibly discomposed. ' 'T is then a question,' said he, ' whether or no this great sum of money would not be better laid by a while until a more promising occasion ? '

" ' 'T is a question, certainly,' I said ; for I began to perceive his drift.

" 'It might be well,' pursued my conspirator, eying me, ' to bestow it meanwhile in some safe hiding-place : doubtless you know of such, Captain ? ' 216

" 'It might, truly,' I said.   'But is it not safe where it now is?'

" 'No, by no means,' said Manning, with conviction.   'And the sooner you and I get to shifting the gold the better,' says he, getting up.

" ''T is in the house, then?' I said.

" 'That you will see,' he answered; and by that I knew it was.

" 'There is just a point, Mr. Manning,' I observed.   'This money, properly expended now, might it not work the success of the plot which we know must otherwise fail?'

" He seemed to reflect a moment, then shook his head.

" 'The chance is so inconsiderable,' said he, 'it is not worth the risk.'

" 'Faith, but I think it is worth it,' said I.

" 'That is for me to decide, by your leave, Captain,' said Manning, blackening.

" Then I smoked his trick.   Had the Cavaliers been in a fair way to success, he would have given me the money in pure speculation, hoping to be rewarded hereafter by the king with a good place about the Court.   But as, on the contrary, they seemed in the way to fail, his game was to nab the gett himself. He could not transport the treasure alone, and so I was to assist him — to get knocked on the head from behind for my pains, belike! The money, then, was not his own; therefore it belonged to Mr. Phelps; and I had next to discover whether Mr. Phelps had designed this gift for his Majesty, or Manning was robbing him. So I pulled out a pistol and covered Mr. Manning.

"'Put forth hand to sword or pistol and I will break the bone of your arm with a bullet,' I said. 'I am tired of this talk. Come, sir! I bear the king's commission; and in that service I have toppled a many more pretty gentlemen into the dust and the dark than you have ever passed the time o' day with. There is better company than you are accustomed to keep, belike, waiting for you on the other side Styx. As God's my life, ye shall join them ere I count five, sith you do not straightway deliver me up three thousand pounds, peaceably and without treachery.'

"I began to count, one, two, but my gentleman was nothing dismayed, and had the impudence to grin at me. Your Manning is a courageous chuff, and 't is pity he is so double-minded and unsteadfast.

" ' Easy, Captain,' says he. ' Easy with the firelock, they are ill engines for mountebanks to handle. Y' are not upon the king's highway, nor am I a fool of a burgess to be scared by your windy violence. If you shot me, you would never find the treasure, o' my word.'

" ' — Three,' said I. ' You forget, sir, I could ask Mr. Phelps.'

" ' You could so,' says Manning, ' and sith the Mayor is a bitter Roundhead, I leave you to imagine the response you would get.'

" ' So y' are about spoiling the Egyptians, is 't not so ? I do begin to perceive a kindred spirit in you,' I said.

" ' Put down your pistol, then,' said Manning ; and so I did, for it had served my turn.

" ' Come, Mr. Manning,' I said, ' time wastes, let us understand one another without more ado. Had the king been on his way to Whitehall, the matter would have worn a different complexion, I take it ; but as his Majesty is fast in Holland, and extremely likely to stay there, we need not discuss that aspect of the problem. As it is, you want the gold for yourself, I know that. Why, therefore, deny it ? Moreover, as you cannot steal it without help, you hoped I should have assisted you blindfold. That will not come to pass ; but I will assist you — upon conditions.'

"Manning looked at me, and I saw that I had hit him.

"'You make a strange mistake, Captain Jacobus,' says he, biting his finger. ''T is a natural suspicion for a gentleman of your habit, or I should think you meant to insult me. We cannot all be highwaymen. These moneys belong to the king, sir.'

"'Ay, sir,' I said, 'and so doth this realm of England ; but he hath it not in his pocket any the more for that. I know what y' are drumbling at. Y' are thinking I am hand and glove with young Langford, because I carry the three seals that he had from the king. I suppose ye guessed he had them, as king's messenger ; and it is true I took them from him. I keep the roads of the West Country as y' are aware ; and I stopped the gallant on his way hither from Lyme Regis, and made him turn me out his pockets for a jest, — for I take nothing, only from Roundheads. The three seals took my fancy ; they smelled of gold to me ; but my gallant would tell me naught about them, till I bound the boy to a tree and tied a piece of lighted match betwixt his fingers, when he found his tongue. He held you in some suspicion of treachery, it seemed, which methought would be the better for me ; therefore I took the adventure on myself, and let little Langford go on his errand. But we had best be quick, for he is but ridden to Fording-bridge to warn the Hampshiremen, and will doubtless be here presently.'

" Manning swallowed that invention of my Minerva like a common gull.

" ' You said — upon conditions ? ' quoth he.

" ' Half,' I said.

" But Manning could not stomach that, and huffed, swore, looked big, and blustered.

" ' Well,' said I, ' I thank God I can earn

my livelihood without picking the pockets of
honest burgesses. Give you good-den, Mr.
Manning,' and I made as if to go.

"At that he altered his note, and presently
agreed ; and we went into the hall, where he
pressed the spring, opened the panelling, and
entered the priest's hole. 'T was a tiny square
stone chamber, with a round window high up
to the left ; on the right a flight of steps led up
to a fireplace, where was a space big enough for
a man to sit with comfort ; and a little door
opened therefrom, I supposed into the chimney
of the hall fireplace. The panel door was
stoutly barred and thicknessed ; a space was cut
out behind the face of the portrait, and a little
slip of canvas moved on a pin, so that a man
could lay his cheek at the back of the thin board
and peer through the eyehole. 'T was a sweet
place wherein to stow money-bags ; and well it
was for Master Phelps that he hath you to his
son-in-law, Anthony ! Manning went up the
steps, kneeled down, and began to grope on the
stones. I whipped out of the chamber and
shut-to the panel quietly ; but he must 'a' heard
the bolt click, for he flung himself against the

wood, crying out. Had he thought instead of the door in the chimney, 'a might have escaped; but I climbed swiftly up and drew bolts on the hither side, and a mighty sooty job it was. Well, there was my clever conspirator fast by the heels till you came to turn him out and cut off his head, Anthony. I am sorry you left it on his shoulders. 'T was your quarrel, and I thought you would like to end it yourself, else I would have killed him. Then I bethought me of Mrs. Barbara, and walked upstairs to search for her, whereupon I heard a little noise of sobbing behind a locked door, upon which I knocked. ' Who 's there ? ' asked some one, in a weeping voice. ' I come from Mr. Langford,' I said. ' My name is Jacobus.' Mrs. Barbara opened at once; and when she saw me, she smiled through her tears," said Jacobus sentimentally.

" You were a figure to make the cat laugh, with your fine lendings and your soot," said Mrs. Barbara. " But I was glad to see you, too. I was afraid for my father, for I made sure there was fighting in the town. And Mr. Manning was not the pleasantest house-mate."

" All things considered," pursued Jacobus, " I thought 't was safest to take Mrs. Barbara from harm's way until matters were settled in the city. Besides, Manning was in the house, and when you came, there must have been bloodshed. So Mrs. Barbara packed her valise while I got her a palfrey ; and, taking her nurse behind me, we sought refuge in my private sanctuary. So endeth the adventure of the three seals ; " and he tossed me the paper. It lies before me now as I write, torn and discolored, one antique head cracked across the cheek.

" Captain," I said, " I am inexpressibly beholden to you," and I reached him my hand.

He shook it negligently. " I doubt me if the king would make quite the same observation," said Jacobus.

XV

A QUESTION OF CONSCIENCE

THE next day came one of the Captain's beggar-spies with news, saying that a general jail delivery would be holden at Exeter on April 18th, when Sir John Penruddock and his following would be put upon their trial; and that Chief Justice Rolles had returned to London, instead of proceeding to Exeter. We learned afterwards that he refused to sit in judgment upon the men who had spared his life; whereupon Cromwell deprived him of office, and sent down a new commission of oyer and terminer. There was never any weakness of sentiment about the Lord Protector's dealings.

"I fear 't is a hanging matter," said Jacobus; "but whatever may befall, I shall ride down and see th' affair through to the end. Also I have a score to settle with Captain Crook. What say you? Shall we take the road again?"

"I am with you," said I.

It was therefore settled that we should start on the morning of the 14th April, three days hence, which would allow four days' easy travelling for the distance.

There are halcyon pauses in life's march, when one steps aside out of the dust into a piece of Eden, and lets the world go roaring by a while unheeded; when the fights and follies of the past drop from us like Christian's pack o' sins; when the unsure and dark future is forgotten. Thus it befell with us for three sunshiny days at the Beggars' Chapel. But upon the eve of my departure, having prepared my equipage for the morrow, I sought Barbara with a heavy heart, leaving the Captain polishing his pistols and whistling, gay as a bird, —

"No man sings a merrier note,
Than he that cannot change a groat,"

chanted Jacobus; but I did not think so.

I found Barbara a little way in the forest, where a bank, matted with creeping blue flowers, hove out above a valley; beyond the tall trees on the opposite ridge the evening sky was painted in scarlet and gold, and, overhead, great rose-colored clouds melted into the blue.

"Barbara," I said, "this will never do. Alas! you and I must part, my dear. To-morrow I ride down to the west (for I am a sworn volunteer) where my life is in jeopardy every hour; and after I must seek my fortune overseas; for I doubt not that what the Captain says is true, that, after this outbreak of the Royalists, the Protector will put in force the most stringent and oppressive ordinances against the Cavaliers. I will come back to you if I live, my dear; but meanwhile I do not hold you bound to me by so much as a word; y' are free as air. For I cannot ask you to marry me."

I had conned this speech with much care, and it pained me a good deal to deliver it; altogether, I felt very solemn and grieved. Therefore I was greatly taken aback when Barbara laughed in my glum face.

"You men think yourselves so mighty wise and heroical!" said she. "I would have you to know, sir, that I am an heiress, and can marry whom I please. What if I chose to marry you, Mr. Anthony Langford ? ''

" I shall have to say you nay," I said, turning aside. " It would not be fitting. You know I could not do 't.''

" Oh, you have the finest feelings in the world, and the most delicate scruples, I know that very well," retorted Barbara, totally unimpressed by my dignified attitude. " But supposing you were to think of some one beside your noble self, sir, for once, — just for a singular novelty.''

" Do I not ? '' said I.

" No, sir, you do not," said she. " Oh, you men ! For a finikin convention, a fantastical whim of honor, you would sacrifice not only yourselves, which would be the less important, but others, no matter who or what. How does it signify which of us hath moneys ? — 't is the weariest commonplace ! Do you suppose a woman sacrifices nothing to take a man's earnings ? You say we have no notion of honor ; well, at least we own a conscience ; wherein, meseemeth, we enjoy a somewhat singular advantage.''

A Question of Conscience

I knew not what to answer, being torn asunder and bewildered.

"I would not ask you twice, were you the Great Chan!" said Barbara, gently, in a little.

There was that in her voice which broke down my resistance. The fortress capitulated; the besieger took possession once and forever.

"Listen to me," said Barbara, presently, "I have a plan. We will go to Virginia and buy an estate with my dowry. Make no mistake, my pragmatical gallant, you shall lead no rose-leaf existence. When we are rich, and if there be a Restoration, we will come home and live at Langford Manor."

We opened the matter that evening to Jacobus, the crafty in counsel.

"I think y' are well advised," quoth our Odysseus. "Faith, I see not what else ye can do, unless ye take to the road like me. And as for that, I doubt if thou wouldst ever make a great hand at it. You will fight and bully when y' are stirred up to 't; but ye take a most prodigious pole and the devil of a lot of stirring. The root of the matter is not in you. Ye do not love the hard living and hard riding, the continual jeopardy, the staggering turns of fortune , — when a man may be carousing with a king's ransom in his pockets one day, and the next fleeing for his life like a fox. Why, look you," pursued Jacobus, warming, " y' are hunted out of house and land, and yet ye have no lust to hunt the hunters. Y' are out of law, ye have naught to lose, and all Christendom lies open before you, Roundheads, fat with ill-gotten gains, jogging to and fro on every road, and swarming in every town. Yet the prospect leaves you cold. 'T is incredible. 'Slife, the Parliament did to me what the Protector hath done to you, before I was your age ; and the Puritan crew have been paying for 't ever since, year in and year out, in blood and gold ; the price is not paid yet ; and so long as I can sit a horse, I go a-questing to fill up the measure that is never filled. Ay, did my own mother stand in the way, I would ride over her face ! "

He gnawed his mustachios and fell silent. I had never seen him so moved ; doubtless my case had brought the remembrance of his own wrongs freshly to mind, when he lost more than house and lands. Barbara looked across in the

firelight, at the dark, lined visage ; Jacobus
caught her glance, his face changed, and presently we fell to discussing how our project
might best be effected. It was finally arranged
that Barbara (whom her father had appointed to
fetch in the morning) should return to Salisbury
to make her preparations, while we rode to Exeter ; thence, as it was unsafe to show our faces
in Salisbury, we were to ride to the village of
Over Wallop in Hampshire, which lay on the
road from Salisbury to Southampton, where Mrs.
Mariabellah Curle dwelt with Mrs. Beatrice and
Dean Young. There Barbara and Mr. Phelps
would meet us ; the Dean should perform the
marriage ; and after we would travel to Southampton and take ship thence to Virginia.

"But will Mr. Phelps agree to this pretty
scheme ? " I asked Barbara.

"Do you think I cannot manage my own
father ? " quoth she. "Besides, he will marry
again, so soon as I am gone, and I shall not be
missed. He hath had a very fine woman in
his eye (to use his own phrase) this ever so
long."

So, while the most of my fellow-Cavaliers lay

bound in prison in fear of death, and a hundred families were suffering the cruel torture of suspense, destiny seemed shaping my way to happiness supreme. But the shadow of others' misfortunes darkened my own fair prospects; why should some be taken and others left? and that which befell them might befall us, some day.

"Y' have won a most admirable lass, boy," quoth the Captain, when Barbara had gone to bed. "A most sweet and praiseworthy wench, Anthony," said he, shaking his head.

That was true; and after all, what did the rest matter?

XVI

THE EIGHTEENTH OF APRIL

ASTROLOGERS have told us that the destinies of man are interwoven with the course of the stars ; a thing at once difficult to believe and hard to disbelieve. Certainly there have been fateful times and days, whose recurrence has been rare as the slow unalterable revolution of the zodiac. Even Cromwell himself, who was so firmly persuaded (in his more perfervid moments) that he was no more than the tool of a lively and interfering Providence, wrought all his greatest deeds on his lucky date of the third September ; whereon also he was born, and whereon he died.

In the same manner, it seemed to me that the eighteenth of April was certainly charged with evil significations. 'T was the date King Charles had first fixed for the Penruddock rising ; and his messenger, baffled by wind and wave, only arrived in time to disorder all arrangements. Now, upon that very day, the leader of the insurrection and the most of his party were put on trial of their life. And in my own case, no sooner had my wedding been devised for the same day, than dire misfortune fell upon me ; and at the time I should have stood at the altar rails (I scarce could think of it) there was I wedged cheek by jowl with that wild freebooter Jacobus, in the dense crowd that packed to bursting the Guildhall at Exeter.

The Guildhall was an arched chamber, great and wide ; the brackets at the springing of the arches were carved into caryatides from the bestiaries ; and at intervals along the cornice were stuck painted armorial shields. Across the upper end ran the dais, where Judge Nicholas, in scarlet and ermine, sat in his great chair to judge the men who had but yesterday spared his life (for Nicholas had been the fellow of Chief Justice Rolles at Salisbury); on either side of him were seated some gentlemen of the county, among whom was Steel the Recorder. Below, upon the Counsels' benches, between the dais and the prisoners' dock, sat Attorney-General

The Eighteenth of April

Prideaux and Sergeant Glyn. In the dock stood Sir John Penruddock and twenty or thirty of his following, among whom I recognized some of my own men, laborers on my estate.

The commission of oyer and terminer having been read, and the usual formalities concluded, the Attorney-General stood up to read the indictment of high treason. The prisoners were then asked to plead guilty or not guilty. Whereupon Penruddock, who was spokesman throughout, disputed the legality of the indictment itself, and demanded counsel to conduct his case. This request was refused him, and he was again required to plead, on pain of having sentence passed then and there. "If I plead, shall I have counsel allowed me?" asked Penruddock. "The Court makes no bargains," returned the Attorney-General. The rest of the prisoners here persuaded Penruddock to plead not guilty, which he did, and again demanded counsel, which was again refused him.

"Sir," said Penruddock, "*durus est hic sermo*, 't is no more than I expected from you; but rather than I will be taken off unheard, I will make my own defence as well as I can."

We also had come with sad enough expectations ; they began to be confirmed ; and thenceforward, throughout the whole five hours occupied by the trial, we endured the spectacle of a brave man foredoomed, but fighting to the last.

The jurors were then called ; there were five-and-thirty of them, out of whom Penruddock challenged twenty-four. Thus the jury entered their gallery a man short ; and it was characteristic of the whole proceedings that the irregularity was considered too trifling to remark upon. All the prisoners except Penruddock were then marched out, leaving the Colonel to take his trial alone. The jurors being sworn, the indictment was read out once more, and Penruddock was asked if he had any exception to make, whereupon he repeated his former plea, that the prosecution was illegal *in toto composito*. This was his impregnable defence throughout ; just as his sacred Majesty Charles First confronted the regicides with the unanswerable proposition that there was no law in existence under which he, the King, might be arraigned. " There can be no treason against a Protector," said Penruddock.

The Eighteenth of April

The validity of the plea was again denied by Recorder Steel, who was moved by sheer malice to take part in the case, for his legal status did not entitle him to address the. prisoner ; and Sergeant Glyn, a tall, sharped-faced man with slanting eyebrows, rose and said : " Sir, you are peremptory ; you strike at the government ; you will fare never a whit the better for this speech. Speak as to any particular exception you have to this indictment."

Penruddock replied that the enactments concerning high treason referred to the King, for whom, and not against whom, he had acted ; if there were any statute authorizing his indictment, he requested to have it read. The Attorney-General answered that Penruddock had not behaved himself in such a manner as to incline the Court to grant favors. At that, Penruddock demanded it as his right, and upon this being refused him, renewed his request on behalf of the jury.

" Sir, the jury ought to be satisfied with what hath been already said, and so might you too," said the Attorney-General.

" Sir, I thank you," returned Penruddock,

"you now tell what I must trust to;" and, indeed, it was plain enough.

The Attorney-General, a dark, bullying fellow, with a red curved nose, then made a large speech, aggravating the offence, falsely stating that Penruddock had been four years in France, when he held a correspondency with the King his master, whom Mr. Prideaux sacrilegiously described as a debauched, lewd young man; that Penruddock had endeavored to engage the nation in another bloody war; and that if he had not been timely prevented, he had thus destroyed the jurors and their whole families. At this point the prisoner interrupted the glib counsel for the government.

"Mr. Attorney," said he, "you have been heretofore of counsel for me; you then made my case better than indeed it was; I see you have the faculty to make men to believe falsehoods to be truth too."

"Sir," retorted Prideaux, truculently, "you interrupt me; you said but now you were a gentleman!"

"I have been thought worthy heretofore to sit on the bench, though now I am at the bar," returned Penruddock, and allowed the Attorney-General to complete his bitter, nonsensical speech, and to call witnesses.

Then Penruddock spoke again. "Sir, you have put me in a bear's skin, now you will bait me with a witness." He turned half round, scanning the faces of the silent crowd in the body of the Court ; then, raising his arm with a sudden, imperious gesture, Penruddock cried out in a great voice : "But I see the face of a gentleman here in Court — I mean Captain Crook — whose conscience can tell him, that I had articles from him which ought to have kept me from hence!"

A little to the left of where we were sitting, Crook rose in his place ; a huge, heavy-shouldered black-avized man ; his face went the color of clay, and his glass-green eyes glistened like a cat's eyes in the dark, as he stared at his accuser. Every head craned to look at him ; there was a rustle and motion as those behind stood up, then, for a full minute, a breathing silence. Penruddock leaned back against the rail of the dock, his dark face frowning and smiling at the forsworn captain of dragoons, who stood dumb as a beast before him. Twice Crook essayed to speak; then he put his hand to his throat and sat down without uttering a word. A murmur went up from the people, as Penruddock turned his shoulder and looked at Judge Nicholas. He had won his case in that moment, had not the jury been packed, and had not Cromwell sent down his lawyers with orders to hang the malignants. But the craven judge held down his head over his notes; when Penruddock appealed to him he answered never a word. 'Twas a pitiful exhibition; a straw mammet would have administered as much justice, with infinitely more dignity.

Jacobus at my side crossed over his right hand and clasped the hilt of his rapier, bowing forward a moment; then he sat upright again with a composed countenance. Some days afterwards I asked him what it was he did; and Jacobus told me that he then took an oath upon the holy Iron, swearing by God and the Mother of God to slay Crook before the week was out. Most persons, I suppose, would have been content to make a quiet resolution to cut the Captain's throat at a good opportunity without this splendid formality; but Jacobus liked to order his little affairs with all the pomp obtainable.

The Attorney-General then called, as witness, Dove, the lachrymose Sheriff of Salisbury, who did no more than complain that Penruddock's men had handled him with violence, one of them "running him through the side with a carabine" — an impossible feat. Other witnesses having been called, some of whose evidence went against the prosecution, proving that Penruddock, besides proclaiming the King, had likewise proclaimed the Protestant religion and privilege of Parliament, the Attorney-General made a second speech, in which he directed the jury to bring in the prisoner guilty.

Penruddock then began to address the jury in his own defence; if Captain Crook, said he, had never promised him pardon in exchange for his surrender (upon which supposition the Court was proceeding), why had Crook, in Penruddock's presence, recounted the circumstance to his commanding officer, Major Butler of Salisbury, adding that he had refused money offered him by Penruddock to fulfil his conditions. For Penruddock, finding Captain Crook unsteadfast and mercenary, had proffered him a bribe of five hundred pounds, which was doubtless what Crook had at first intended he should do, but, in the event, found it more profitable to forego. Immediately upon his refusal, some of the troopers, having gotten wind of the affair, mutinied, and were disbanded "for defending these conditions of ours," said Penruddock. "But let that pass, and henceforward, instead of life, liberty, and estate, which were the articles agreed upon, let drawing, hanging, and quartering bear the denomination of Captain Crook's articles!"

There was a brief noise of applause at the back of the Court; and, turning, we perceived it arose from a knot of red-coated troopers; doubtless the honest soldiers in question. Penruddock then went on to enlarge upon his original plea with an excellent eloquence.

"There can be no treason but against the King; the law knows no such person as a Protector. . . . Gentlemen, look upon me, I am the image of my Creator, and that stamp of His which is my visage is not to be defaced, without an account given, wherefore it was. . . .

The Eighteenth of April

The law which I am now tried by is no law but what is cut out by the point of a rebellious sword ; and the sheets in which they are recorded, being varnished with the moisture of an eloquent tongue, if you look not well to 't, may chance to serve for some of your shrouds. . . . You can at most make but a riot of this,'' he concluded. "Consider of it, and the Lord direct you for the best."

The jury then left the Court ; soon after they were gone, the great clock of the Cathedral chimed three-quarters past four, and, after an interval incredibly tedious, they entered again as it tolled five, and gave the verdict, guilty.

"The Lord forgive you," said Sir John Penruddock, solemnly, "for you know not what you do."

The mockery was over ; all rose to leave the Court. It is a matter of history how that on the Monday following, Sergeant Glyn sentenced almost all the prisoners to death ; that some were afterwards reprieved and sold in Barbadoes, while three or four were acquitted ; and how Sir John Penruddock and Sir Hugh Grove were beheaded at Exeter on May 16th following. 243

Jacobus and I pressed through the dispersing crowd, and about half-way down the High Street fell into step one on either side of Captain Crook. Jacobus rounded him in the ear.

"Crook, y' are a damned villain," said he, in a low voice. "Do not raise your voice nor attempt to escape, or we will stab you out of hand. I challenge you to a fair duello. I have no time for punctilios and preliminaries, nor, I take leave to say, are you so much the gentleman as to stand upon so much ceremony. Settle your weapons here and now, and appoint a place of meeting for to-night or to-morrow betimes."

Crook turned a dusky visage quickly upon us in turn ; but, perceiving that resistance was dangerous, he merely quickened his pace.

"What the devil is this insolence?" he demanded. "And who are ye?"

"That is nothing to the purpose," quoth Jacobus. "'T is sufficient for you to know that I am a man that hath taken a fancy to fight you, will-ye, nill-ye."

"Am I to take up the quarrel of every common stabber? I would have you to know I fight but with gentlemen, sir," said Crook.

The Eighteenth of April

" Y' are but a poor liar," returned Jacobus.
" Ye trepan honest gentlemen to their death
with your bloody treacheries and false Articles.
Y' are more forsworn than any pitiful shilling
perjurer at Westminster, Crook of Woodstock.
Come, sirrah, I have no time to waste upon
such dogs as you ! Where shall I soil my sword
with your vitals ? What spot of earth shall I
defile with your blood ? "

The man was quivering with rage ; but it
would have required a brave man to free himself
from two such assailants : and Crook, I take it,
was a coward in grain.

" I will not answer you," said he, with a
great assumption of dignity. " Ye may send
me a cartel and ye will, as one gentleman to
another, to my quarters at Rougemont yonder ;
or ye two foot-pads may come seek me, and since
y' are so fain, ye may try conclusions with the
whole corporal's guard. 'T is my last word."

" Why, very well," returned Jacobus, indifferently. " Go and hide in thy Castle. 'T is
pity your great general Fairfax broke the port-
cullis in his godly zeal ; you should ha' slept
the sounder else."

We had reached the foot of the long hill at the top of which stands the ruined Castle of Rougemont, where, however, there was still accommodation for Captain Crook and a corporal's guard. Jacobus stopped, whereupon Crook set off at a very lively pace of walk. We walked slowly across the road to a side street ; but no sooner were we round the corner than we ran like hares, doubling and twisting back to our inn. "For," said Jacobus, " no sooner is our gentleman in his Castle than he will send his soldadoes to catch us." But if he did, we saw nothing of them.

" Ye will ride to-morrow betimes, of course, Anthony," said Jacobus, as we sat gloomily over our wine that evening. " There is no more for you to do here. The play is played out."

" Why, what are you going to do?" I inquired.

" I have my affair with Crook to settle," replied Jacobus. " But that is a piece of business I can best perform alone."

" For how many men do you take yourself?" I said. " Crook will never go out wanting half-a-dozen dragoons at his heels. Are you going to carry Rougemont Castle by yourself?"

Jacobus was plainly nonplussed; and for my part, I could not imagine how the two of us were to accomplish his purpose, much less how he could perform it by himself; for that Crook would not fight was certain.

"For God's sake," cried Jacobus, angrily, "go and get married, and leave me to mind my business."

"If I have a mind to stay in this city," I returned, "it is not you who shall hinder me. I take an interest in its scenery and the curiosities. Come! I am not going. Now we can debate with a quiet mind. It appears to me that y' have proposed the impossible. But I raise no exceptions, not I."

The Captain looked at me from under his brows, pulled his mustachios, and relapsed into silence.

"Without a mighty hard push for 't, we shall be no more than accessory to our own ruin," he went on, presently. "After the mortification we put upon the excellent Crook, he will be raising the devil's own hue-and-cry after us; the town constable will be set upon our track; and Crook himself, belike, is even now searching the streets with a lantern, like the heathen philosopher of the ancients, and with a handful of dragoons to help him. We are caught in a trap; 't is two against a city; and the odds strike me as cruel disproportionate."

"Well, we have no time to recruit a regiment," I said. "Before the bottle is out, Crook may be bursting the doors upon us," and an ugly presage flitted across my mind. I saw the row of the condemned on Tyburn Hill, writhing in the noose; while the hangman, aloft on the crossbar, stamped on their shoulders, until, one by one, they dangled motionless and limp.

"I could do with less than a regiment," said Jacobus. "Give me but a file of Haslerigg's Lobsters, or Lunsford's Horse, and I would sweep the streets with Crook's dragoons, 'twixt prime and noonsong. By God," he cried, slapping his hand on the table, "I have it! The disbanded troopers! Y' heard what Penruddock said in Court."

"What then?" I asked; and Jacobus proceeded to expound a project ; 't was but a desperate chance ; but we were driven to such a pinch, that we took speedy resolution upon it.

"Once more, Anthony," said Jacobus, rising to buckle on sword and pistols, " I ask you, a' God's name, to take horse and get you gone. Y' are merely foolish to remain ; 't is no more than the indulgence of a freak, when all's said. As for vengeance, until Noll and the regicides are drawn quick and hanged, there can be no useful vengeance. For me, I set not my life at a groat's value, save for the pleasurable excitement of risking it. But here are you, with a sweetheart awaiting you, and a long life afore ye ; 't is murdering posterity to fling it away. And conceive with what face I should carry tidings of your death to fair Mrs. Barbara ! No, no, take horse and be wise, Anthony."

" Were she here, she would bid me go with you," I answered.

" I would not make too sure of that, neither," said Jacobus, with a grin ; and although my sentiment had the right sound to 't, upon a second consideration, I had my doubts also.

"Well, I am not going, at any rate, as I said before," quoth I.

The Captain, seeing that my mind was set, desisted from further argument ; and, armed and muffled, we set forth to discover the disbanded troopers.

XVII

THE LAST NOTCH ON THE SCORE

WE must have visited a round dozen of alehouses without finding the men we sought; passing from the windy and dark streets into the bright tap-rooms where a crew of mechanics and 'prentices loudly debated the day's events over pipe and ale-cup. The tavern talk ran always down the same gutter; hatred of the Protector's bloody Army, and the Protector's bloody scriveners; and at the same time, condemnation of Penruddock for attempting to upset the orderly state of the country, under which trade so prospered.

"The cowardly shop-folk," said Jacobus, "they would see every yeoman and gentleman in the country put to death before they stirred a finger, unless their money-bags were in danger. Comes me your Puritan, with pike and shot, bellowing religion; and straightway, by your leave, they are all good Puritans; and you shall see, when the King returns, they will be lighting bonfires in every street for pure joy; and Geneva gown and bands may pack to sour Scotland, where they be ever welcome."

As he spoke, we entered an alehouse in a bystreet, and spying through an open door that led from the tap-room into a little parlor beyond a group of men in scarlet seated round a table, we went in upon them.

Sure enough, there were three of the troopers we had observed in the Court-house: one, a great ox of a man, with a brick-red countenance, purple-jowled with shaving; another, stalwart and long-limbed, with a dark eye as alert as a fowl's; and the third, a lean man with a great hooked nose, a brown goat's-beard, and something of a fanatical air.

"God save you and all of us," said Jacobus. "Are ye of Captain Crook's company — mine old acquaintance, Bully Crook?"

The Captain spoke with a kind of patient heartiness; he had assumed, in a twinkling, the voice and manner proper to the part he was to play, — that of a peaceable, quiet, country gentleman living for his crops and his beeves, yet meekly willing, at a word, to sacrifice all for friendship's sake.

"Once upon a time, but now no longer so," quoth the big trooper, in deep, rumbling tones, slapping his pewter ale-pot upside down.

"What!" cried Jacobus, lighting up like a candle. "Are ye then among those noble hearts of whom Sir John Penruddock did speak in Court to-day? who for conscience' sake, did risk a halter; who rather chose the reproach of Egypt than the praise of iniquity?"

"That was it," said the dark-eyed man, in a dry voice, looking at us with a face of wood.

"Landlord!" cried Jacobus, kindling into a sort of gentle ecstasy, "a jack of ale for these gentlemen. I am proud to make your acquaintance, friends; I would have you to shake my hand. Right so! when I said damned Crook was mine acquaintance, you must not take it he was ever my friend. No, no. For, truly, he is mine enemy. See now, sirs, what a fortunate conjunction is here! Behold how the hand of God bringeth honest men together at a pinch! Although I am of the contrary party, I

say so; y' are honest men, and I care not to
cloak my principles; for I, have I not gotten
me religion? The King, say I, for God surely
made him; but Bishops, away with them!
Give me your Bishop, and I will spit in his
face. But let that pass. What have I to do
with Crook, or he with me, saith 'a? Why
now, I will tell you. Heard ye what Penruddock said in his speech, how that Crook, after
refusing moneys proffered him to carry out his
articles, put a pistol to Penruddock's head and
threatened to shoot him, did not the noble Colonel promise to betray a certain Royalist into
his clutches? But noble Sir John stood fast;
and word was brought to me of the incident —
for I was the Royalist in question, friends all;
and for that I am well-to-do, did Crook covet
to get me in his clutches. Ay, I have moneys;
the Lord hath prospered me : why should I
deny it?" And Jacobus, with a simple, smiling, open countenance, slapped his pockets till
the coins jingled. The men had taken their
pipes in their hands and were regarding him with
grave attention.

"And what dost here, sir, in the very tents

o' the Amalekites, as a man may say ? " growled the big trooper.

" Canst ask ? " returned Jacobus, " when mine old friend and comrade John Penruddock standeth in peril of his life," the Captain's voice declined upon a sob, and he brushed his sleeve across his eyes. " 'T is but little I may do, belike ; but here I stand upon the chance of it, in spite of the devil Crook. He did espy me to-day, and would have taken and laid me in ward, but that he had no soldiers with him ; yet he threatened me, and meseemeth 't is very like I shall presently figure in the dock, cheek by jowl with the rebels, — I, John Blechynder, than whom the Lord Protector hath no more peaceable subject, — and my nephew here beside me, — " Jacobus put his hand on my shoulder — " in the very blossom and May-day of his youth, — all that Crook may dip his dirty hand in my coffers. For we will not leave poor Penruddock while we may render him the least particle of service. What ! Are we not his friends ? Hath he not hazarded his life for us ? " and a freshet of emotion again overwhelmed this noble spirit.

The troopers seemed somewhat at a loss; they stared at us in silence; when the big trooper's glance, wandering for a moment, lit on the black-jack, and, filling his cup from it, he passed it on.

"Your excellent good health, sirs," said he; the others followed him, and we drank to them in turn; after which we seemed to stand upon a better footing of understanding.

"Had I but half-a-score tall men such as you at my back," quoth Jacobus, "I would not care for vermin such as Crook that much," and he snapped his fingers and leaned back, smiling.

The three men exchanged glances; and the fanatic-looking trooper clasped his bony hands loosely before him on the table, opened wide his great pale-blue eyes, and, gazing into vacancy, began to speak. His comrades watched him with an evident admiration.

"For lifting ourselves into your service, sir, to deal plainly with you, 't is mainly a matter of wages. Doth God take care for oxen? Yea, truly, as saith Holy Writ; yet until His kingdom on earth be established, His saints must still shift for themselves. For that you look for a king, excellent sir, y' are so far in the right, so do we ; y' are but wrong in that ye fix your hopes on the Young Man Charles, who is but a lewd person, a notorious evil-liver, whom may God confound. Yea, verily, there is but one Reign to look for, —— the Reign of the saints on earth, the thousand years of triumph, the Fifth Monarchy, the absolute dominion of God !" He spread his arms abroad and his voice rose. " Pope and kaiser, priest and king, shall bow down, bow down, shall crouch and fawn beneath the iron rod. Corruption and darkness shall flee away, and the whole earth shall be clothed in the light of the morning. The noise of wars shall be utterly silenced, and the crying of the poor and needy be no more heard in the land. The strongholds and high places of cruelty shall be laid even with the dust, and grass shall grow upon their battlements. To bring these things to pass we labor mightily : we take the sword ; we lie dogging at our prayers until our eyes be dim ; we serve mammon for righteousness' sake. Yea, for this did we not choose to serve under Crook ;

and did he not cajole us with lying promises, saying that he himself was a Fifth Monarchy man, and that he used his commission but as a means to hasten the coming of the kingdom? — hoping, without doubt, to cut out some deal of wealth for himself by means of our swords. 'T was naught to us whether the malignant Penruddock lived or died : but there were moneys to be gotten from him ; he did offer Crook five hundred pounds for liberty ; yet did Crook start aside like a broken bow, preferring the favor of Cromwell before the glory of the Lord. Wherefore did we admonish this glazing Judas, using great plainness of speech in the matter ; but he, being stiff-necked and utterly delivered to Satan, broke out into a mighty heat of anger, commanding our dismissal. How long, O Lord !" The preacher twisted his fingers in his beard, turning up his eyes. "Silver and gold must go to the foundations of the city of the kingdom," he went on, in a high monotone. "Her walls shall be of precious stones, and her towers of rubies. The wise and learned shall dwell therein ; to them shall come all the nations of the earth for wisdom. But we be unlearned and ignorant men, fit only to wield the sword ; what can we do save hew therewith the corner-stones for the habitations of the just ? . . . Pay us, therefore, and we will serve you ; even as the builders of the Temple wrought with sword on hip.''

The man paused and wiped his forehead ; for he had been speaking with a vehemence that made the glasses ring. In the momentary silence that followed, there came a clatter of hoofs and jingling of bridles in the street, and we heard the outer door flung open.

Jacobus leaped to his feet. "Crook, by God!" he cried. The big trooper heaved himself up, and opened the door as the latch clicked. Jacobus and I whipped against the wall, whence we could espy Crook through the crack of the door.

"What, Gilroy !" said he. "Stand aside, sirrah, stand aside, or I will put a bullet in your head. I am about searching the house."

Gilroy, who was girt with a great broadsword, drew it with such suddenness that Crook leapt back a pace to avoid a blow.

"Out o' this, Beelzebub," thundered the

trooper. "Or, by the Twelve Tribes of Israel, I will chop you into gobbets ! Y' are no better than a dead man, Crook ! Call your men," he bellowed. "Call 'em in, man, and behold and see if they will draw sword on brethren-in-the-Lord."

We heard the outer door clap, and the trample of retreating hoofs. Gilroy rolled in again, shutting the door upon the astonished folk in the tap-room, filled his tankard, drank it off, and regarded the Captain with a grin.

"How now ?" said he.

"'Sblood," said Jacobus, "mighty well done ;" and, taking out a fistful of coin, he bestowed it on Gilroy ; and, spreading a handful of gold-pieces on the table, "Handsel," said he. "A crown [1] a day for every day I do remain in Exeter, and a jacobus each at parting, to serve me as body-guard. What say you ? Shall we strike a bargain ?"

The country gentleman, having served his turn, had vanished in a twinkling ; and Jacobus, himself again, upright, alert, with a valiant eye

[1] The regulation pay of a trooper was two shillings per diem.

and the port of a commander, stood in his place.
The men stiffened to attention as if upon parade,
and saluted.

" Why, very well," said Jacobus. " Let
me know your names."

The preacher gave his name as Robert War-
renwell; the burly Gilroy was christened
Joshua; while the third man was known as
Skillard the Rider. The Captain ordered them
to hire horses (Skillard, it seemed, possessed a
nag of his own), and to present themselves at
our inn at nine of the clock the next morning.

When we returned thither, we found the
lights out, the shutters up, and the door barred;
but, upon knocking, the landlord himself opened
instantly to us. After locking and bolting the
door again, with the most particular care, he
took the candle in his shaking hand, and surveyed us. The hoary, fat old man looked as
though he had seen a spirit : his lips were trembling, his cheeks fallen in, and his eyes wild.

" What the devil ails the man ? " asked
Jacobus.

" Zurs, zurs," said the innkeeper, " who be
ye to bring a old honest man's house into dis-

repute, and his life into danger! 'T was ill done, zurs, 't was ill done. I had sooner than forty pounds I had never set eyes on ye. Life-lekins! Have I lived through the civil broils to be hanged on account of two bloody rebel-lious Cavaliers," he wailed.

"Come, come, sirrah, keep a civil tongue, and explain matters," said Jacobus, sitting down on the table.

"Explain! 'T is for you to explain, I d' think," returned the old man, querulously. "No zooner do you be gone out o' house to-night, than a half-a-company o' dragoons, or thereabout, cometh tinking o' horsebarck down street, and 'a stampeth in and arxes for landlord. 'I be he,' says I, whereon Captain putteth pistol to my head and saith he, 'Hast a couple of Cavaliers lodging here?' says he, ''T is a hanging matter, I warn ye,' says he; 'for they be two bloody conspirators against Government.' 'Swouns, not I,' I says. 'Whutt be loike, then,' I arxed him. 'A middle-sized man wi' a long nose and a devilish countenance,' 'a saith, 'and a girt yoong man above sax feet o' stature, wi' a red face and no be-ard,' says he. 'Swounz,

The Last Notch on the Score

Captain,' I says. 'I do believe that two zuch did coom in to drink a toss o' Hollands about five o' th' clock, and out again,' says I. 'Which wai did they goo,' arxed he. 'I marked them not,' I zed; whereat he cursed me up and down, and trampled all over houze, he and his soldiers. 'If y' 'ave lied,' 'a saith, ' you shall swing for 't, by God. Give me a cup of Rhenish,' and 'a drank it down and went away, and never paid a groat. Zurs, get you gone, I d' beg and pray of ye; and the Lord forgive ye that ye ever coom anigh a old man as never did ye any harm.''

"What, man!" cried Jacobus, "pluck up heart. Y' are not hanged yet, nor never will be, I 'll wager. Y' have done the best day's work as ever in your life; y' have saved the lives of two o' the King his Majesty's most precious subjects, and ye shall not lose by that. Content you : we will ride betimes to-morrow. Now reckon up the score, and set a price on thy alarums.''

Something pacified, the innkeeper ciphered out the score in chalk upon the panelling ; and Jacobus (who must have made mighty profita-

263

ble use of his time during my absence overseas)
paid him double.

" God save you," said our host, completely
consoled and beaming. " By 'r Lady, y' are
two of the prettiest civil gentlemen as ever I
served o' my life. Hark ye, zurs," said he,
creasing his face into innumerable wrinkles, " I
would, wi' all my heart, the King, God bless
him, were to come home again, and the bloody
Army and their General at the black devil.
Zed I to Captain, ' Swouns, not I,' I says,"
and the old man was taken with a fit of chuckling ; and, going upstairs ahead of us to light us
to our chamber, he kept repeating, with an infinite zest, fragments of his momentous conversation with the baffled Crook. " ' Hast a couple
o' bloody Cavaliers lodging here ? ' arxed he.
' Swouns, not I,' says I ; " and when our host
closed the door behind him, we could hear him
chuckling still as he stumped down the passage.

The morrow was to bring forth the last of
my adventures with Jacobus, — a final pitch of
the dice with Fortune ; before the sun had set
we should have cut ourselves free of the coils of
conspiracy, or another's sword should have

freed us entirely from earthly doings. The thought of it ran in my dreams all night, with a clash and sparkle of swords; and now the balance dipt one way and now another. Once Jacobus and I, our enemy slain behind us, and trouble at an end, would be riding swiftly through the mellow dark towards a golden dawning; and again, I would be smitten with a sharp stroke, taste the agony of death, and be suddenly filled with the despair of loss irrevocable.

But I awoke with the chiming of bells in my ears; 't was no more than the Cathedral clock striking; nevertheless, I took it as a good omen, and sprang up, fit to face the world.

Jacobus was slumbering on his pallet like a child. Under the magic touch of sleep, a subtle change had passed upon his face; something had gone from it; and, instead, something of the man's inner spirit that smouldered beneath the rough fabric of robbery, fighting, and antic mummery of which his life was made up, peered forth. I stood a paternoster-while perusing the time-scarred countenance, but I had no eyes to decipher it. Had I not been my mother's son, perhaps I had not perceived so much as I did. I wondered idly whether there lived the woman who could have read that inscrutable gallant, crafty, generous riddle Jacobus the Highwayman, Sir Clipsely Carew the Cavalier. I know now that such an one there was ; and that she was dead.

Unwilling to arouse Jacobus, I leaned my elbows on the sill, thrusting head and shoulders out of the open casement. Our room was a garret chamber, and the window commanded an ascending field of roofs, brown thatch, or red, shining tiles, with the smoke drifting and curling from the chimneys ; beyond the huddled houses rose the great, broken rampart of Rougemont Castle, over which white clouds came lifting in ranks, with now and again a flying wisp of gray vapor like a puff of smoke. The wind bore odors of the country mist, with a briny tincture from the sea ; and, presently, there came the thin shrilling of a trumpet. Captain Crook, in Rougemont Castle, was sounding boot-and-saddle.

A few minutes later, armed and equipped, we were devouring a hasty breakfast ; and, before we had finished, hoofs rang in the street, and our whole army drew up at the door. We contemplated the troopers through the window, sitting in the saddle like statues, carbine on thigh, and toes turned in ; perfectly equipped in bright steel cap, gorget, back and breast, great boots and winking spurs ; the horses groomed to a marvel, the sun gleaming upon glossy haunch and shoulder.

"Had I a hundred times as many, there would be doings," quoth Jacobus, with his mouth full of pasty.

The landlord, fidgety already as a hen with ducklings, could scarce contain himself at sight of this new portent, and saw us forth with benisons, and, I doubt not, the most pious inward thanksgivings.

Jacobus took his place on the right front, as Captain ; while I rode upon the left, in the senior corporal's position.

"Rank entire. Right wheel. Forward," shouted the commanding officer ; and we paced, jingling, down the street and wheeled into the High Street.

From the Castle on the hill-top sounded the

Tuequet (warning for a march); a minute
later, from out the shadow of the Archway
issued a flash of steel and scarlet; and a knot
of horsemen, with a black-bearded man at their
head, came riding down the hill towards us.
Jacobus halted instantly. Fortune, in hastening
the event, was already befriending us. We
were abreast of the court-house, I remember,
with its arched and columned front designed in
the Italian manner. The people in the street
began to stop and stare, but took us, of course,
for Crook's own troopers. So, doubtless, did
Crook himself; for, until he and his four men
were well within pistol-shot, he did not appear
to remark us. Then I saw his face change
suddenly. Crying " halt," and reining up
his horse, he whipped out a pistol and fired.
Jacobus swerved, and the ball struck upon the
plated breast of Joshua Gilroy, and glanced off.

" What, ho ! brethren," roared the trooper.
" Wouldst see old Gilroy murdered. Seize
the traitor, brothers."

But before the words were out of his mouth,
Jacobus had flung his pistol in Crook's face and
was charging down upon him with naked blade

The Last Notch on the Score

uplifted. Swift as his assailant, Crook had
drawn his sword ready to strike, but the fury of
the onset caused his horse to rear, and his blow
fell harmless. With a level sweep of his sword
Jacobus cut deep into the dragoon's neck, just
above the stiff collar of the buff coat, and the
man swayed and toppled sideways. I spurred
up to Jacobus' side, and for a moment we
both fought desperately with Crook's troopers.
But our own soldadoes pushed into the fray,
shouting to their comrades to desist, and dealing
great blows with the flat of their broadswords.
There was a mighty din and confusion, and
holloing and running together of people; and
our assailants began to give back. Perhaps they
were not entirely desirous of taking us; at any
rate, although blows were falling like hail, I
saw no one hurt; and Gilroy and Skillard were
grinning broadly above the chin-strap. Jacobus
backed his horse out of the press; I followed
instantly, and, wheeling, we struck spurs in and
galloped full tilt down the street and out of the
East Gate.

The wind whistled past our ears, and the
horses settled into their stride; we thought we

were clean escaped; when we heard the drum of hoofs behind us. Looking back, we saw Skillard the Rider, on his huge bay stallion, gaining on us at every step; I have never seen such a devil of a nag as he rode that day. There was no use in racing, and we drew rein in the little village of Heavitree, and stopped at the alehouse. Skillard came up at a full gallop, pulled his lathering horse on its haunches, and saluted. Methought the situation was a trifle difficult.

"Y' have a good nag," remarked Jacobus. "Will you sell him?"

"Not I, sir, by your good leave," returned the Rider. "You see he is mighty useful on occasions."

"And why the devil are the other men not here?" demanded Jacobus, fiercely.

"They await orders, Captain," returned Skillard, eying him. "This is a pretty business. There will be a noise."

"'Sblood," said Jacobus. "The orders are, Dismiss. I have slain your backsliding murdering Captain, you see; wherefore go to, go rejoin your company. Y' have done very well,

The Last Notch on the Score

for a parcel of bloody Roundheads. Here is wages, all as agreed, is it not so? With a piece or so for liquor. Give you good-den, till we meet again, as may befall, for I am often on the road.''

The man, still staring, murmured a word of thanks, took the money with an air of great dubiety, and saluted mechanically as we rode away. Looking back, we saw that he had wheeled his horse, and was still gazing after us, the sun beating down on his mailed figure, and the steam from his horse going up in a cloud about him.

XVIII

THE INEVITABLE

'TWAS on a Friday that Jacobus and I quitted Exeter, and by Monday evening at sunset we were riding into Over Wallop village, having travelled by way of Winchester, where (borrowing moneys from Jacobus) I had gotten me wedding attire, and the ring, which the Captain, with his customary gratuitous effrontery, insisted on purchasing from Mr. Jedediah Dickenson.

The village lay among meadows and groves in a fair and rich country; the rooks were leisurely sailing and cawing above the trees; the bells were chiming to evensong; the light air enfolded the place like a dream; and, after the grief and the turmoil, 't was like the entrance into a charmed land. Dismounting in the Rose Garland, we exchanged buff coat and

The Inevitable

boots for doublet and buckled shoon; and, our host informing us that 't was a Saint's Day, and that as his reverence the Dean would be reading prayers even now, doubtless his household would be at the church, we set off thither. The city had lately risen, it seemed, upon Cromwell's Independent, and kicked him forth to hammer his spiritual pots elsewhere, so that the Dean once more enjoyed his living. The weather-stained, tiny church, with lichened roof and square tower night-capped with red tiles, stood upon a knoll, secluded among trees; a clump of yews, on either side the path, rooted among the bones that lay beneath the crowded, bricky tombs, interlaced their branches and made a dusky vestibule to the little porch, so low that we must doff our hats and stoop.

We entered and sat down near the door. Barbara, with Mrs. Mariabellah Curle and Mrs. Beatrice, kneeled at the bench fronting the chancel; an upright, little, white-haired clergyman in surplice and scarlet hood was reading evening prayers; there was no one else in the building. As we crossed the threshold, Barbara turned her head and looked at me a moment across the

18   273

golden dimness that filled the place, and a fancy
came into my head that her swift glance was
the division, thin and trenchant as a sword, set
between the old life and the new. The parson's voice ran musically in my ears, and I fell
into a muse; Jacobus, to whom the forms of
devotion represented an etiquette due to Church
and King to be strictly performed upon occasion, kneeling devoutly resolute beside me.

I beheld, with a sort of pitying contempt,
the long, stupid, happy, ignorant years of the
youth who, wrapt in sweet illusion, walked
gayly up and down a pleasance, dreaming that
its pleached hedges circumscribed the world;
until within the past month, when fate, forcing
a sword into his hand, had flung him neck and
heels into the world's actual, calamitous battlefield, where death winds always in and out, and
the crying of the wounded mingles with call of
tucket and roll of drum, to reckon, for the
first time, the price ambition pays, and to
count himself singularly fortunate if he might
no more than guard his honor unchipped throughout the mêlée. The future stretched before
me in the image of the uncharted sea upon

which we were about to set sail, that broke so immeasurably far away upon the shores of a perilous wilderness, whither I was bound with one beside whose welfare I weighed my own as a grain of dust; for a single freezing moment I contemplated the whole possibilities of that appalling enterprise, then took hold upon it with what hope and resolution I could muster; and the benediction brought my meditations to a fit conclusion.

Our greetings over, we all went to sup at the Vicarage, where we found Mr. Phelps, rosy, jolly, and bursting with good humor. We made the oddest party: the three prettiest ladies, I vow and swear, to bless God for, in all broad England; a Dean, a Highwayman, a Mayor, and an outlawed Cavalier; nevertheless, 't was the pleasantest and the most festivous meeting in the world. The Dean and his ladies made us mighty good cheer; we exchanged the tale of our adventures; and the long evening went by like a peal of bells. When we were about to take our leave, Jacobus produced two small leathern caskets from his doublet, and, holding them in his hand, deliv-

ered himself of the following romantical state-
ment.

"My excellent friend and comrade, Mr.
Anthony Langford, hath of purpose omitted
one particular in his relation of the conversation he was privileged to hold with His Most
Sacred Majesty the King," began Jacobus, with
such an air that the ancient, tapestried room
became at once transformed as it were into a
Royal antechamber; while we ourselves felt
that we were actors in a state ceremonial. The
ladies rose and courtesied, the very moment the
Dean and his worship the Mayor stood up. I
looked at the orator in some astonishment, for I
had omitted nothing in my recital, — nothing,
that is, that was meet for ladies' ear; but,
catching the slightest contraction of his eyelid,
I composed my face to an intelligent gravity.
"Our Royal Master," went on Jacobus, with
solemn relish, "hath never forgot the slightest
service rendered to him by the least among his
subjects; yet hath he a spirit so rare and kindly,
and withal of such subtle discrimination, that oft
he alloweth a loyal deed to go unrecompensed,
thus bestowing upon the doer the high privilege

of serving him with a zeal unalloyed by mercenary considerations. Thus, when Mr. Langford had the honor to recount to His Majesty the generosity of Mrs. Mariabellah Curle and Mrs. Beatrice Young in coming to the relief of his messengers in their extremity, with the gift of a horse, — a service that might — although it did not — that might, I swear, have gained a kingdom, — the King, I say, charged Mr. Langford with the following message. 'Tell Captain Jacobus,' saith His Majesty, 'to seek out these ladies, and to say to them that their sovereign in exile lieth under an infinite obligation to them, that 't is his saddest misfortune to behold his loving subjects' devotion unrequited, and his chiefest consolation that they are proud and fain to serve him for nought. Request the Captain, also,' so went the message, — 'request the Captain to convey to Mrs. Mariabellah Curle and to Mrs. Beatrice Young these trinkets — '" Jacobus opened the cases, and took from each a jewelled bracelet — "' and to inform them that the King craves their acceptance of these trifles, as a token that, at least, His Majesty is

not all ungrateful,' " and Jacobus clasped a bracelet on each white wrist.

The ladies flushed and exclaimed with pleasure, and kissed the Captain heartily on both
cheeks; which, indeed, he deserved, for 't was
a neat device for providing the bridesmaids'
presents in a manner most pleasing to them; a
matter which had exercised me sorely, for in
my miserable destitution I could afford none.
Certainly the Captain enjoyed exceptional opportunities; for when the girls handed me the
trinkets to admire, I discerned the maker's name
graven inside, J. Dickenson, Winchester.

"Madam," went on the Captain, turning to
Barbara with a profound bow, "'t is not the
usage for a wedding-guest to come empty-handed
to the marriage; I crave your pardon for so
doing; but the gift I had the honor to design
for you is something cumbrous, so that for convenience' sake I did despatch it to the care of
Mr. Phelps's agent in Southampton."

Whereupon Barbara kissed Jacobus also; and
soon after he and I repaired to our inn. When
we came to open the heavy iron chest on ship-
board, we found it stuffed full of silver-gilt and

silver plate, — a gift fit for a princess, — all marked J. Dickenson, Winchester ; whence I concluded that 't was Mul-Sack's booty, which the Captain had somehow discovered and confiscated. 'T was a sweet revenge upon me, although at first I marvelled that a King's officer should utilize his privileges for private benefaction ; but presently concluded that the Captain had set it down as no more than a just remuneration for my services. For long I scrupled to tell my wife the history of her wedding-present ; and when I did so, she thought it an excellent jest, which (I remember) surprised me at the time.

During the evening Mr. Phelps handed me a letter, superscribed to myself, which, he said, had come with his own mails from Flanders. As it elucidated more than one mysterious matter, I read the epistle aloud ; and here subjoin it.

COLOGNE, AT THE SIGN OF A PEACOCK IN A CIRCLE.
Eleventh April, 1655.

SIR, — This is to inform you, at the King's desire, as I knew your address (though I would

willingly have written of my own intention) of
certain singular disclosures which have lately
come to light at the Court of our Royal Master
here in Cologne, in case a knowledge of the particulars thereof may stead you towards the regaining
of your estate, that was so treacherously lost, of
which you did tell me when we had the happiness to converse together on shipboard. Your
false friend, Mr. Manning, of whom you spoke,
whom all here set down as no more than a pragmatical empty busy-body, hath been, it now
appears, playing the common spy since the day
of his arrival. He came hither at first and with
a letter of introduction from Dr. Earles, his uncle,
and prating much of his friendship with my Lord
of Pembroke, endeavoring to insinuate himself
to become the King's Privado by every day taking
him the " Duernal " to read, which he regularly
received from London ; and in this he so far succeeded that His Majesty, from regarding him
simply as his " Paper-boy " (as he said), presently
allowed Mr. Manning to mix himself in the unhappy Penruddock business. Upon hearing of
the latter's sad conclusion, the King returned
immediately to Cologne ; and, a day or two later,
Manning, who had been absent no one knew
where, also returned thither. But, in the mean-

The Inevitable

time, the King had received a letter from the
Earl of Pembroke, in answer to one of his, saying that Manning was a loose person of no reputation whom he had discharged from his service.
Whereupon His Majesty's suspicions were
awakened ; and hearing moreover that Manning
received letters continually from Antwerp, and
had letters of credit upon a merchant there, he
despatched a trusty messenger to intercept his
mails. Thus, no sooner had Manning returned
with his accustomed confidence, than this man
came to the King bringing the mails of three
posts, which, being opened, were found to contain letters and instructions from Cromwell and
Thurloe to Manning, and fabulous disclosures of
imaginary plots from Manning to the government, with requests for more money. For a
thousand crowns Manning offered to put them in
possession at last of the whole of the particulars of
what he was pleased to call the Plymouth Plot, of
which, said he, he spoke when he was last in London, which we found in the later of the three mails.
'T was a sweet design for the surprise and taking
of Plymouth ; a vessel with five hundred men was
to come to certain creek, and, upon sign given,
such a place in the town should be seized upon by
some, whilst others should possess both fort and

island. At the same time were to arrive — and I am come at last to what concerns you, dear sir — gentlemen at the head of land forces of volunteers, Sir Hugh Pollard from Devonshire, Colonel Arundel and others from Cornwall, and Mr. Anthony Langford from Wiltshire — "of which dangerous and subtle malignant I did warn your Excellency at our last meeting —" This ingenious rascal, Manning, who, I profess, is a most accomplished scribbler, did even describe the council held by the King when this famous plot was resolved upon, touching smartly upon His Majesty's gestures and behavior. Upon this the King did send two of his servants to seize upon the caballer's person and papers, who took him in Flagrante Delicto, in his chamber writing postdated letters, with his cipher before him, and put him in ward, where he now is. He loudly declares his innocency, saying that he saw no harm in writing particular relations of what never happened; that, in fact, he was doing the King a service, in that he turned the attention of the government from the true course of events.

I hope the discovery of this man's double falsity may chance to avail you with the brewer; and if it should fall out so, I am heartily glad to have been of service to you; but I fear me that

Noll is little likely to relinquish what he hath once clawed hold of.

For myself and my wife (who desireth to be heartily remembered to you) we are certainly dwelling amongst persons of sense and quality, and should, I do suppose, count ourselves happy; yet life is at present one long Duello, for these gentlemen of the Court, from my Lord of Rochester — I dare not say the K——g — to the vile Cheffinch, all cherish the same singular delusion, that a man's wife is every one's property but his own.

I am, sir,

> Your most obedient and willing friend to serve you,
>
> RICHARD HUMPHREYVILLE.

But the "singular disclosures" came too late to be of service; for, after the Penruddock affair, Cromwell would use scant courtesy to Cavaliers for some time to come.

The next morning we were married. 'T was a day of sunshine and chiming bells and emotion, of flowers and farewells. Jacobus was to ride with us to Southampton; and, so soon as the service was over, we three took horse at the churchyard gate. All the village was gathered together in holiday attire; and, looking back, we saw the bright, motley crowd waving their hats, and listened to the noise of cheering that mingled with the gay clamor of the bells. In the shadow of the lich-gate stood the Dean in his robes, and the sturdy, gray-bearded figure of the Mayor, gazing after us, and the two ladies, fluttering kerchiefs.

Three hours or so of riding brought us out upon the downs above Southampton town, with its thicket of ships' masts fringing the edge of the broad, sparkling water. Jacobus reined up, and, dismounting, went up to Barbara, hat in hand, with a bow.

"Farewell, Mrs. Langford," said he; and I think the new sound of the title gratified both wife and husband. "I wish you all prosperity." He would have kissed her hand, but she gave him her cheek.

"Come down and sup with us, man," said I, "or at least crush a bottle before we part."

"Not I," returned the Captain, mounting his nag. "I have business toward. The freebooter bids you adieu, my son."

"Jacobus," I said, "y' have done me very

much kindness. Tell me, why did you so? Are my manners and conversation so engaging? I should like to think it."

"Do not flatter yourself," he answered. "I have only to remember that I am an old friend of your family, as it were. I knew your mother ere she was married." His glance left mine, rested upon Barbara for the fraction of a second, and came back again. I looked aside, for 't was like spying on a man's secret unawares.

Jacobus held out his hand; I grasped it, and we parted in silence; for I could not think upon the words I wanted. So my wife and I rode forward; and when I looked back, Jacobus was gone.

THE END.

PRINTED BY JOHN WILSON AND SON AT
THE UNIVERSITY PRESS IN CAMBRIDGE
DURING   MAY   M DCCC XCVI.   FOR
STONE AND KIMBALL
NEW YORK

www.ingramcontent.com/pod-product-compliance
Lightning Source LLC
Chambersburg PA
CBHW020848020726
47497CB00005B/1308